SAFE

AT

HOME

BY

PAULA BOTT

Scobre Press Corporation
2255 Calle Clara
La Jolla, CA 92037

Scobre Press books may be purchased for educa-
tional, business or sales promotional use.

Edited by Ramey Temple
Illustrated by James Mellett
Cover Design by Michael Lynch

ISBN 1-933423-27-7

TOUCHDOWN EDITION

www.scobre.com

CHAPTER ONE

THE FIELD

"Get in a line everyone. Let's pick 'em." My brother Joe pointed and shouted, directing traffic as he tried to organize the group of noisy boys surrounding him. "Let's move, the sun goes down in two hours."

Playing, and winning, on "The Field" meant everything to us back then. Most of the neighborhood kids would find their way to the Field pretty much every day. We'd play for hours. Sometimes we'd play Home Run Derby, sometimes we'd have fielding practice, and sometimes, when enough kids showed up, we'd play real games. When the score was close, which it almost always was, we'd stay out until the darkness blanketed our smiling faces. By the end of a long afternoon, the moon and the streetlights barely shone upon the ball as it hopped through the infield or soared into the air.

The Field was a strip of beat-up grass located across the street from our apartment. The area was about one quarter of the size of a football field and it was poorly maintained. Weeds poked through the choppy sod like warts on a frog's back. Big holes made the most agile of runners look clumsy while trying to stay within the baseline, a challenge that was rarely met.

Despite the odd dimensions and lame conditions of the Field, most of our free time was spent there. Its closeness to so many of the neighborhood homes combined with the shaded open space drew a swarm of local kids. Finding any vacated area in the southern region of Arizona was difficult, especially in our little town. I lived with my mother, father, and two older brothers in Tierra de Sueño, which, when translated from Spanish to English, means *dreamland*. Our apartment was on the second floor, behind a tall wooden fence that acted as the border on the left field foul line. Hitting one over that rickety fence always counted as an automatic out because it usually meant that we'd lost another baseball. The hitter got his punishment by having to climb the splintery barrier to try and fetch the ball. The ball almost always ended up hidden deep in the bushes that separated the fence from our apartment.

Out of necessity, right field included a section of the street. Teams always had to place one or two outfielders near the foul line depending on the amount of cars parked there. Although it didn't happen often, a cracked windshield or a dented car door made for a quick end to an exciting game.

Despite the odd boundaries of the Field, there was nothing that compared to the feeling you got when the center of the bat connected with the heart of the ball. Yet, to be successful, you couldn't always swing for the fences. You had to learn to time your swing just right so you could drive the ball to center, the only portion of the Field that allowed for a home run. If you hit the ball too far or long down the left field line, you were picking splinters out of your hands from climbing the fence. And if you sliced it too hard to right field, you were counting your allowance money to pay for car damage.

When I made my way into the field I usually played center. As a center fielder, my heart would race when I snared a line drive in the webbing of my glove, or threw a perfect strike to home plate, nailing the runner dead in his tracks. Chasing down fly balls in the pothole-infested outfield required a lot of skill. Playing out there was the only time I didn't mind the guys referring to me as a ballerina, tiptoeing gracefully around potholes and in between cars.

The outfield was uneven and unkempt, but was located far enough away from screaming line drives and scorching one-hoppers to make the few kids who were afraid of the ball feel pretty safe. Only the bravest of the boys brought their gloves into the infield. Ground balls on the Field bounced around like a fly trapped in between a screen and a window. "Danger," and "dentist" were two buzzwords for anyone positioned in front of the baselines.

While the brave ones lined up in the infield, only the very best players lined up in right field. That was the sole spot on our neighborhood turf where errors weren't tolerated. Like a hockey goalie swallowing up a puck, right fielders on the Field had to guard parked cars from flying baseballs. Most of the time that job included bracing a hip on the car's side door and leaping or lunging in whatever direction the ball was headed. A bad play from a right fielder was disastrous.

Although I was never asked to play right field, I wasn't concerned about getting not being picked to play either. I was probably right about in the middle of the pack in terms of skills. My oldest brother, Jose, who we called Joe, organized most of the games and would usually stick me in center field. Even though I was the only girl on the block, Joe and my other brother, Carlos, got me into most games. I was a short and skinny nine-year-old girl, but they knew I was athletic and tough. I had the cuts, scrapes, and bruises to prove it. Being the youngest, the smallest, and the only girl out there never slowed me down. In fact, I think being the underdog made me fight twice as hard.

But on this particular day, I wasn't even given the chance to compete. Home Run Derby was the game of the day, and Joe, my know-it-all brother, pushed me away. He stuck out his bony chest and raised his chin arrogantly, his jet-black, flattop hair shining in the sun. "Sorry, Selena, today is only for the big boys. Maybe tomorrow." He dismissed me without a second thought, turning to the crowd of boys. "Come on guys, line up and let's pick 'em." Joe looked up at the sun once more to remind the noisy crowd that they were racing against time.

I looked over at Carlos, hoping he'd plead my case. Carlos usually treated me better than Joe, but when we were out on the Field, he always went along with our brother's tough guy attitude. Surely, the fact that Carlos was four inches shorter and thirty pounds lighter than our big brother had something to do with this. My next option was to run home and tell Mom what had happened. I knew she would make it all right. But she was working downtown, cleaning houses for some rich people. I was stuck at the mercy of my brothers and I didn't know what to do.

My mind raced as I stared at the big rock that sat on the edge of the Field. It represented the only visible landscape in the otherwise desolate area. It served as a backstop for our bizarre-shaped diamond. The boulder towered over me, and it had a crevice in its side that looked like a set of big lips. A year earlier, Cole and Micah, the boys who lived next door, had colored the gap with red spray paint, making it look like bright red lipstick.

As the boys finally formed the line that Joe had commanded, they began to choose teams. I jumped up on top of the big rock behind them, sat down, and dangled my feet over the side where the lips showed. The boys continued to pick teams, unfazed by my attempt to get their attention. I desperately tried to think of a way to get into the game as I chewed on my fingernails. On top of that giant rock, I felt like a queen on a throne. And I started thinking like one. A few of the boys below me looked up to see what I was doing. I twisted my thick, black hair around my index finger as my mind raced. With each thought my short legs swung faster and faster across the pretend lips. Within a few seconds I had devised the perfect way to make sure that I would get a chance to play.

I pushed myself off the rock and landed feet first in the thick clump of grass in front of the boys. Although I ran toward them, they still tried to ignore me. That is, until I made a challenge that changed everything.

"I bet I can hit the ball farther than you, Joe." I spoke loudly, pointing at him in front of everyone. This comment immediately drew the attention of the entire crowd. "Well?" I said, putting my hands on my hips.

"Ooooh." Sergio Lopez shot a sharp look at my brother, trying to egg him on. "Now that's a challenge, Joe."

"You get one pitch and I get three," I continued. "If I lose, I won't bug you to let me play ever again, but if I win, you have to promise that from now on, I always get to play!"

After I had spoken those words I wanted them back. What if Joe hit the ball farther than me? He *was* the best player on the

Field, after all. If I quit now, I would probably get the chance to play tomorrow, or the next day. But if I lost, would I ever get the chance to play on The Field again? I had to take back my offer. "Wait, Joe, I—" my voice quivered and then stopped.

"See, I knew it," he said. "Now you're being smart, Selena. You don't want to play against me."

His cocky attitude made me want to scream. I couldn't back down now. "Yes I do." I moved to about three inches from my brother and stood on my tiptoes, in an attempt to look eye to eye with him. "Unless, I mean—" I grinned.

"Unless what?" He prodded.

"Unless, you're too scared—too chicken." I raised my eyebrows at my brother and laughed as I said, "Are you too chicken, Joe?"

I could see that Joe was fuming now. Sergio looked over at him and started flapping his arms up and down, imitating the movements of a chicken. "Buck, buck, buck, buck, buck!" I heard a few other boys jump in.

I smiled as I twisted and fiddled with the ribbons and bows that Mom had strewn through my hair. Even when I didn't come home looking like the poster child for a laundry detergent commercial, I had to have my nightly hair washing. Each morning before school, she would take the time to put ribbons in my hair. Every time I got nervous or excited about something I would run my fingers through the ribbons and I could almost hear Mom's voice saying, "Mi hija, you can do anything you set your mind to." Mi hija is an endearing way, in Spanish, to say *my daughter*. Mom always called me that.

"Buck, buck, buck, buck, buck." Carlos joined Sergio.

6

"Shut up, Carlos." Joe shot a tough guy look over at Carlos, who quickly went mute. Joe then moved closer to me, whispering so that only I could hear. "Okay, Selena, but just remember, you asked for this. It's time I teach you a lesson, little girl." Joe glanced at the crowd of about fifteen boys who were gathered around us at home plate. "Let's play ball." He smiled nervously again, knowing deep down that this was not a winning situation for him. On one hand, he could not turn down my challenge in front of all these people, especially after all the chicken stuff. But if he accepted it, and beat his baby sister, whom he was more than a foot taller, he would still look foolish.

Then, there was the unthinkable. He *could* lose.

Feeling the pressure of the situation, he addressed the crowd once more. "I'll even bat left-handed, to give her a chance." Everyone smiled at this show of sportsmanship. The truth was, they were all secretly hoping that Joe, the biggest and oldest boy on the Field, would lose.

I reached down and grabbed the smallest aluminum bat from the pile of five. From experience I realized that being the youngest had one distinct advantage—I got to go first. I loved a challenge, but I thrived even more off the chance to put pressure on my opponent. I dug my dirty white tennis shoes into the lumpy grass and barked at Joe, "I'm ready." The group of boys stood a few feet behind me at home plate as Joe marched over to the pitcher's mound.

He lofted the first pitch softly into the air and my uppercut swing sent the baseball looping high, but not far. Shoot. That wasn't going to do it. Even left-handed, my brother would be able to hit the ball farther than that. "That was just the first one." I explained to the crowd. "Give me another one, Joe."

The second pitch was a bit inside and the ball weakly bounced off the handle of my bat. That one was even shorter than my first swing. Joe was really smiling now, knowing that if I didn't make good contact with this next pitch he would beat me very easily, *and* do so left-handed. "All right, this is it. Now I'm serious." I said, trying to convince myself. The crowd settled back a few feet, obviously disappointed by my first two swings. They knew that there was no chance I was going to beat Joe without an awesome final swing.

I pounded the bat into the ground three times, refocusing. "Keep your eye on the ball, Selena," I told myself. Snapping the bat back into position, I intensely watched Joe's right hand. The third pitch came in a little low, but that forced me to level out my swing. As I extended my short arms, the ball hit the "sweet spot" of my bat and shot forty feet in the air, sailing into center field and rolling another fifteen feet after it hit the ground. It was probably the farthest ball I had ever hit.

I have to mention that smacking a baseball perfectly on the "sweet spot" is probably the greatest feeling in the world. And after experiencing it in front of everyone, I desperately wanted more.

"Whoooa!!" reacted the neighborhood boys who stood behind me.

"Uh-oh, Joe." Sergio laughed and looked over at my brother.

"Big hit, Selena!" Carlos slapped me five.

I raised my right arm and pointed at the ball. "I think that's a winner! But you better leave it there just in case the "Incredible Hulk" gets lucky."

The look on Joe's face reflected his nervousness, but he tried to mask it, lifting his head high. "Give me any bat. It doesn't matter."

Sergio tossed him the "Big Barrel," the bat known for its fat head. "Show us what you've got, Joe."

Joe flipped the bat awkwardly over his left shoulder. He took a few practice swings, but each one sent the bat wobbling in different directions. He was no switch hitter. Everyone knew that.

"Now, remember, only one swing," I chuckled.

All eyes focused on Joe. Carlos wound up and delivered a pitch in the dirt, which Joe was smart enough not to swing at. "Sorry Joe," Carlos winked at me, letting me know that he was doing whatever he could to help me win. I knew that his next pitch was going to have to be over the plate, or Carlos would really hear it from Joe. Sure enough, I was right. Carlos let go of a straight pitch that headed right down the middle of the plate. As the ball reached the batter's box Joe swung the heavy bat with all his might and connected solidly with the ball. At first I thought for sure that his ball was going to fly past mine. Luckily for me though, the ball connected with the top half of his bat and sailed straight up into the air. It flew like a bird for about seventy feet and then plopped straight down near second base, well short of my blast.

"That was a terrible pitch, Carlos!" Joe yelled in embarrassment as he walked up to Carlos and gave him a shove.

I skipped over to Joe to shake his hand, but he scampered away, finding a spot within the crowd of boys. "Go away, Selana." He acted like a wounded soldier looking for the protection of his troops.

My light brown face beamed as I announced, "Well, looks

like I'll be seeing you guys tomorrow, and the next day, and the next day, and the next!"

Watching my cocky brother wilt was rewarding, but the greatest prize I earned that day on the Field was the respect of the neighborhood boys. After seeing me take on Joe, the biggest and toughest guy out there, everyone agreed that this little girl could play. No longer was I the last player picked on the Field. And, to my surprise, there were no more whispers of, "Just let her get on base." The "pitch underhand to Selena" rule was wiped out, too.

Baseball truly became the focus of my life. Winning that bet with Joe started it all. From that day on, more than anything else, I wanted to be a baseball player.

CHAPTER TWO

A HARD CALL

"Cup check! Cup check!" As a member of the Pirates youth league baseball team I had listened to that phrase for twelve straight weeks—and I was sick of it.

Before every game, Coach Fisher would walk by each boy sitting on the bench and yell: "Cup check! Cup check!" One by one my teammates would stand up and knock on their cups, showing that they were wearing the protective gear. When he'd reach me, the only girl on a team full of boys, instead of screaming "cup check," he'd yell, "gut check!" It sounds silly, but it always got me fired up for the game.

Getting permission from Mom and Dad to be the only girl on an all boys team wasn't easy. After pleading with my parents for about two months, I finally got their attention. When Dad finally caved in and told me that he had signed me up to play baseball with the boys, I nearly jumped out of my dinner chair. I hopped up and down in our kitchen, hugging Dad like I'd just won the lottery.

Mom wasn't quite as thrilled. She wanted me to play softball, and was sure that I would have more fun competing against, and hanging out with, the girls. But I had no interest in Bobby Sox softball, especially after Terry Silva and Pam Sanders told me about their practices. Their coaches actually put little pink stickers on the softballs so the girls would concentrate while batting. Any league where the players *forgot* to concentrate without the help of little pink stickers was not for me. I told Mom this and I think she started to understand why I was avoiding softball. I was an athlete, not some pink princess.

As it turned out, competing against the boys wasn't a problem for me. Growing up with two older brothers who always picked on me made me tougher than most of the boys I played with anyway. And although I was just nine, I knew a heck of a lot about baseball. For starters, there is an entire vocabulary of baseball terms that any decent player needs to know. There are hits, outs, strikes, errors, singles, doubles, triples, home runs, short hops, grounders, pop-ups, pickoffs, grand slams, curveballs, fastballs, sliders, splitters, knuckleballs, spitballs, changeups, screwballs, basket catches, intentional walks, regular walks, last licks, and infield flies. You can strike out looking, you can strike out swinging, you can make a diving stop, and you can even balk, which is really confusing. Everyone on a baseball team has to know how to bunt, when to steal, when to tag up, what the count is, what the sign was, and when to slide. I knew all that stuff pretty well, which was much more than I could say for a bunch of my boy teammates—the same teammates who made fun of me at every opportunity.

Despite being the only she-Pirate, I'd become one of our best players. My hitting really took off with the wide dimensions of a regulation baseball diamond. Unlike the unforgiving measurements on the Field, my deep shots to left and right field were fair game. I also became great with the glove, predicting most of the bounces on the well-groomed fields we played on. Tracking fly balls became easier, too, especially since I didn't have to tiptoe around potholes and in between cars.

To be honest, Mom *was* right about one thing. The social part of being a member of on an all-boys team tempered the thrill I got from the game of baseball. The chatter in the dugout revolved around the latest video games, comic books, collector's cards and skateboards. None of these things interested me. Even if they had, I doubt the boys would have included me in their talks. I don't know why, but having me around really bothered some of them. It was hard, but I tried not to pay attention to their dirty looks and mean comments.

That was the attitude I maintained heading into our final game of the season against the Dodgers. Aside from us, they were the only undefeated team in the league. We didn't have a real playoff system, so the team that won this game would be the unofficial champion of the league. The Pirates ran to their positions, separating like a mob of ants sprayed with water. Garret Carter found his spot in right field without any help, a first this season. Dennis Martinez jumped up and down on third base, a ridiculous ritual he performed every time he manned the hot corner. Tommy Smith had his hat fall off as he ran to second base, an occurrence that had become a ceremonial start to our games.

When I sprinted over to first base, a spot I'd played almost the entire season, I never worried about losing my cap. Before the game, Mom would pull my long black hair through the back of it and tie my ponytail with one of her bright yellow ribbons, which matched our yellow and black uniforms.

During the past three months, I'd become one of the best first basemen in the league. Coach said that I was a natural at scooping the short hops. I knew better. The truth was, I'd been practicing those scoops since second grade on the beat-up grass of the Field. So playing first base and swallowing up errant throws on the perfectly manicured infields we played on was a breeze.

A pop up and a strikeout retired the first two Dodgers to start the inning.

I punched the center of my mitt, encouraging our pitcher, Jacob Rivera. "Here we go, Jacob, right down the pipe Jacob. No batter, no batter, no batter, no batter, no batter." Just as I finished my sentence, their number-three hitter scorched a one hopper to Tommy at second base. He was able to knock it down but his throw to me at first floated to the left side of the bag. Knowing I couldn't stretch my glove that far across my body, I reacted with pure instinct, reaching out my bare right hand to stop the ball. My index finger snapped backward as the ball smacked into the upper portion of my palm with a pop. Luckily, it dropped straight down, keeping the runner from advancing to second base. I shook my stinging hand, hoping the pain would quickly disappear.

Coach Fisher made a quick move out of the dugout to check on my condition, but I waved him off with my glove. "I'm fine," I shouted.

"You sure?" he answered back, raising his eyebrows and looking concerned.

I nodded, not wanting to reveal my pain through a cracked voice. As I bowed my head, I stared at my dusty cleats, hand-me-downs from my older brother Carlos. I recalled all the times I'd been banged up on the Field, including a few barehanded catch attempts. I never quit on my neighborhood turf, and I certainly wasn't going to quit here.

I bent down, placing both hands on my bony knees. I didn't put any pressure on my right hand though, as the burning sensation had yet to go away. Before another thought of pain could cloud my mind, the next batter hit a slow roller back to our pitcher, Jacob Rivera. I looked at the first base bag and ran back toward it, anchoring my right foot on the corner of the white square. Once secured, I turned and looked at Jacob, who threw a bullet into the heart of my glove. The snap of the leather proved to be a much better feeling than the snap of my skin.

I ran into the dugout and dropped my glove on the ground as I headed straight for the water cooler. The fresh water relieved my dry throat. Once I'd hopped up on the far end of the wood bench, out of the view of my teammates, I splashed some water on my stinging hand.

Unfortunately, Jacob saw me. "Oh, did you break a fingernail, Selena?" he teased. The rest of the boys laughed, magnifying my discomfort.

"Did you forget you had a glove?" chimed in Dennis.

I rolled my eyes at them and turned my attention toward the game. This was the way that they'd been teasing me all year long. When it first began, I would yell and scream back at them, but I soon realized that my negative reaction was fueling their fire, making them doubly obnoxious. About halfway through the season Dad sat me down and explained to me that the boys' harsh words were dripping with jealousy. It was bad enough that I was better than most of them, but being that I was a girl made them twice as mad.

15

I knew my barehanded stop was a great play so I didn't need to respond to their stupid comments.

I was able to release most of my frustration when I got up to the plate. Even though some of my teammates wouldn't admit it, I was our team's best hitter and my skills had only improved as the season wore on. By the sixth inning against the Dodgers, I had reached base safely in every at bat, including a home run that hopped past the Dodgers' right fielder.

We led 6-5 going into the top half of the seventh, the final inning. The Dodgers had one at bat remaining. The first Dodger batter hit a little pop-up to our third baseman, Dennis, who broke late for the blooper but ended up making an accidental dive for the catch. The next batter walked on four straight pitches and ran over to second base on a wild pitch.

With one out, their best hitter, Andy Newsome, stepped up to the plate. He rested his bat on the ground as he tried to pull his undersized royal blue shirt over his round belly. He was big and strong, a kid who crushed the ball whenever he connected with the meat of the bat. On the first pitch he swung mightily and missed. The bat wrapped so far around the back of his head that he twisted into the ground like a corkscrew, toppling over into the dirt.

"That's all right Andy," yelled a Dodgers coach from the dugout. "Get this one!"

With his next swing Andy barely connected with the ball, sending a grounder to our shortstop, David Gonzalez. Surprisingly, the ball bounced off the heel of David's glove and rolled toward the pitcher's mound. David hustled after it and threw a low, off-balance laser that tailed toward the first base side of the bag. The speeding ball skipped hard into the dirt, but I was able to stretch to my left and reach my glove down to scoop the ball up on the short hop. Thanks to some major flexibility, my foot managed to stay on the rubber base too. This was a real accomplishment considering I'd played with torn-up rug bases all my life on the Field and had become used to dragging the base with my toe.

I started to stand upright after completing the second out. But just as I lifted my head I knew that I was about to get plowed over. The runner, Giant Andy, as Mom called him when she retold the story to my brothers later that night, was chugging down the line as fast as he could. He tried to halt to a stop but his body sprawled out of control as he crossed over first base. He slammed into my side with his shoulder and rolled over me like a truck smacking into an empty garbage can. Andy's bouncing helmet shot out of a large pile of dust that had formed around us. It was followed by two messy ballplayers staggering to their feet. I sat up on the dirt, dazed and confused for a few seconds. The umpire ran over to us in order to get a closer look. I extended my left hand into the air and, there, secure in my glove was the dustiest baseball I had ever seen. I'd held on to the ball and Giant Andy was called out!

Before I could wipe the dirt off my face, stand up, or stop to check for broken bones, I noticed out of the corner of my eye that the Dodgers' runner, who'd started on second base, was now rounding third and heading home. Still sitting on the infield dirt, I instantly spun around on my behind, snatched the ball out of my glove and threw home with all my might. Although I was throwing from an awkward sitting position, the ball zipped straight toward the plate where our catcher, Thad Hudson, received it and applied the tag for the final out.

Game over! Pirates win!

Coaches from both teams ran to the crash site at first base, picking us up and dusting us off. Giant Andy had a few tears running down his cheeks. I'm not sure if he was hurt by our collision or disappointed that the Dodgers' undefeated season had come to an end—probably a little of both. The small crowd of parents stood and clapped for Andy and me—showing good sportsmanship. I think they were all relieved to see that the two of us were able to walk away from that collision without any serious injuries. After staggering to my feet, I took a moment to reflect on one of the most exciting plays that I'd ever made on a baseball field. Suddenly, I couldn't help but smile through the pain I was starting to feel all over my body.

Coach Fisher bent down and put his arm around me. "Man, talk about a gut check. You okay, Selena?"

"Yeah, I'm fine, Coach," I lied. The *truth* was, Giant Andy had bruised my leg pretty bad. Plus, a chunk of dirt was stuck in my left eye and I'd bit my tongue when I hit the ground. I could taste the blood in my mouth. Still, there was no way that I was going to give my teammates the satisfaction of seeing me hurt.

I stood up and gingerly walked off the field to another round of applause from the section of cheering parents. The boys ignored my accomplishment, of course. Dennis was the first to pick on me. "It looked like Andy was trying to kiss you," he smiled. I wasn't surprised. Upset, yes, but not surprised. My play had just won us the game and none of my teammates had anything nice to say about it whatsoever.

After we shook hands with the other team, I sprinted over to the snack bar, a step behind the rest of my teammates. Mom walked towards me, her lawn chair under her left arm. She'd been to every one of my games this season. Dad worked late hours as a school custodian so he saw only a few. I flipped my duffel bag onto Mom's right arm. "Can you hold this for a second?"

Mom grabbed the edge of the duffel with one hand like a catcher snaring a wild pitch. She put down the lawn chair and swung her other arm around my neck, putting me in a sweet-tempered headlock. "I'm so proud of you. Wow, what a great play!"

I lowered my head, showing my frustration. "Yeah, well at least somebody noticed. I'm so sick of these boys. You should've heard all the stupid things they said to me today. The same junk I've heard all season."

Mom lifted up our dog, Campeóna, to my face. She gave me a big wet kiss on my ear and I started to laugh. Campeóna, which means *champion* in Spanish, had been my dog since I was five years old. She always made me feel happy, so Mom brought her to all my games as a good luck charm. Campeóna was a crazy little white mutt who weighed about ten pounds, although the constraints of her leash converted her from a hyper playmate to a panting, shade-seeking fluff ball.

While giving me a hug, Mom eyed my dusty ribbon. "Let me fix your bow." She carefully put down the bag and chair and tied the fancy yellow ribbon.

"You're one tough cookie." A voice interrupted us from the rear. A stout, balding man with a black colored goatee came within sight. "That was a heck of a play to end the game."

I looked down, embarrassed to accept the compliment. "Thank you." I spoke softly.

"Have you ever considered playing Bobby Sox softball? My two older daughters have played the last couple of years and they really love it. I'm coaching an under twelve team next year and we're looking for players. Boy, we'd sure love to have someone as good as you." The man saw that I was a little uncomfortable. I think he could sense that I didn't want to give up my baseball career. His tone softened. "If you want, I'll get you the information. No pressure."

Mom looked at me and raised her eyebrows inquisitively. I stared back at her, raising my shoulders with uncertainty. Although I had been able to hold my own with the boys physically, playing alongside them as teammates wasn't all I thought it would be. I simply was not accepted. Playing the game that I loved wasn't as fun as it should have been, and I knew it.

"Here's my number." The man handed Mom a business card. "If you decide you want to play, give me a call."

"Thank you." Mom nodded her head in appreciation.

As the man faded in the distance Mom bumped my hip playfully with her hip. "What do you think, Mi hija?"

I wasn't exactly sure what I thought. Mom's eyes looked into mine and I turned away, deep in thought. I glanced at the baseball diamond, at my muddied uniform, and my glove. *Softball games are played on a diamond*, I thought, *and you wear a glove and you can slide just as hard as you can in baseball*. A moment later, I fixed my eyes on Dennis and some of my other Pirate teammates. They were still making comments about me breaking a fingernail and wanting to kiss Giant Andy. I realized exactly what I had to do. I turned my attention back to Mom. "I think we should give that guy a call."

On the car ride home I tried to convince myself that playing softball wouldn't be all that bad. *It's just like baseball*, I thought, *but the ball is bigger and they pitch underhand instead of over-hand. So what? At least I'll be able to hang out with some girls and maybe even make some friends.* I continued trying to convince myself that I was not quitting on baseball.

CHAPTER THREE

A CHANGEUP

As I pulled on my first ever softball uniform, I wasn't overly pleased with the neon orange and black color scheme. That was the bad news. The good news was that although I wasn't playing my favorite sport every day, I'd gained something extremely valuable when I joined the all girls Bobby Sox softball league—comfort.

Switching from baseball to softball was a change I never expected to make, but once I did, I found that it wasn't so bad. First of all, I was ten times more physically comfortable playing softball than baseball. Switching to softball meant that I shed baseball's hot, polyester pants in favor of cool mesh shorts. I also dropped the short sleeve jersey tops of youth baseball for the relaxed, cotton tank tops of softball. And the streamlined visors worked much better than the baseball caps when it came to dealing with my ponytails. Of course, none of it had anything to do with fashion. No. It had everything to do with the scorching heat of Arizona. For that reason, comfort owned a top spot on my list of priorities.

The other major comfort factor was that I was now hanging around other girls. Finally, I had found a team where I actually fit in! Gone were the nasty comments I'd gotten used to while playing with the boys. And although some of the girls on our team were too prissy for me, most of us loved competing and were serious about playing softball.

As I expected, it didn't take long for me to adjust to playing with the bigger ball either. Throwing-wise, I followed Coach's advice and worked on placing my fingers on the laces, giving my small hand a better grip on the larger ball. I found out that playing first base was actually easier in softball than in baseball because the enlarged ball was a bigger target for me to scoop and squeeze in my glove.

On the other hand, switching sports drastically changed my hitting style. I quickly realized that smacking home runs was much harder in this sport because the bigger ball didn't travel nearly as far as a baseball did when it shot off the bat. So I shortened my swing and stopped going for the fences. My new swing virtually eliminated striking out for me. After just a few weeks playing my new sport, I had transformed myself into a great contact hitter with an occasional burst of power. My adjustments worked so well that I developed into one of the most productive batters on our softball team—the Orange Crush. At the age of ten, I'd found my comfort zone in softball.

The biggest change in my game occurred during the second half of my first season on the Orange Crush. One day in practice, I was shagging balls in the outfield and throwing them back to the infield with an underhand windmill toss. I was out there with Kate Jamison, our star pitcher who was sidelined with a broken leg. Kate was a great skier when she wasn't playing softball, and had fractured her femur, which I found out is the largest bone in the entire human body, on a ski trip to Colorado with her family the previous weekend. We were all bummed out for Kate. She loved softball and was able to keep a positive attitude, attending our practices and games even though her season on the field was over. With Kate sidelined, we were one pitcher short.

A high fly ball landed directly in my glove and I threw an underhand bullet through the infield dirt. The laser bounced twice before reaching home plate. "Hey Selena, you're gonna hurt your arm throwing from way out there." Coach Shepard shouted in a raspy voice. He was the balding man who had recruited me for softball at my youth baseball game a few months earlier.

I placed my hand on my hip in a mischievous fashion. "Well, why don't you give me a chance on the mound then, Coach." I was only joking, of course. I loved playing first base.

Apparently, Coach Shepard didn't get a joke when he heard one. A few minutes later he was running toward the outfield grass holding a catcher's glove under his arm. When he reached me, he was huffing and puffing, but smiling. "If you're any good, this could really help us, Selena." He spoke excitedly through deep breaths. "Without Jamie," he said, knocking his fist on her cast, "we really need another pitcher. Let's see if we've found one." Coach paced forty-five feet and crouched down in a catcher's stance. "Okay, show me what you've got."

My heart started to race as the entire team made their way onto the outfield grass to watch me pitch. I gripped the ball in my hand and stared at the catcher's mitt. I looked to my left, then to my right and then straight into the heart of the mitt again. I'd watched

24

Jamie pitch before and I pretty much knew what to do. Set your feet, grip the ball loosely but securely, step forward, cock your arm back and release. So I did.

Right when I let go of the ball I knew that I'd thrown it pretty hard, so that was good. What I didn't know was that my pitch was about five feet higher than my target—Coach's mitt. The softball left my hand and continued to rise until it had soared well over Coach's head, landing in the middle of left field and finally coming to a stop just beyond the foul line.

"Whoops," I giggled, embarrassed in front of all my teammates.

Coach stood up, looked at me and smiled. "Well, you can pitch, you just can't aim." He laughed at his own joke. "It'll take some practice, but I think you can do it, Selena." I figured Coach was just trying to be nice so I forced a small smile and thanked him.

A moment later, Coach Shepard took off his faded orange hat and ran his fingers though the small amount of hair he had left on his head. "Marisa, get some rest tonight, you're starting tomorrow." I breathed a sigh of relief, glad that Coach wasn't thinking about me as a pitcher anymore. Just as I finished this thought he turned to me, "Selena, you'll start at first base, but be ready, because you're gonna come in and relieve Marisa when she needs you."

I reacted confidently by nodding, trying hard to hide my nervousness with a wide smile. I was going to be pitching in a real game! I loved challenges, but what had I gotten myself into? Coach had seen that first pitch. It wasn't even close to his mitt, let alone being near the strike zone. I was definitely going to humiliate myself tomorrow.

As we walked to the dugout my softball teammates smothered me with encouragement. "You're gonna do awesome, Selena!" Anne Fishburn, our shortstop, put her arm around me.

Elizabeth, our catcher, tossed one of her shin guards at me. I could barely catch it as Anne was still draped on my sides. "You know I'll take care of you out there, girl," said Elizabeth.

That night I didn't tell Mom or Dad about my pitching opportunity. I wanted to surprise them. But I did warn them that they couldn't miss tomorrow's game. When I got into bed that night my mind raced thinking about my new assignment. At first, I tried to be really positive. *If I really focus,* I thought, *eventually I'll be able to control my pitches better. I'll learn as I go along, just like I learned how to play first base. Everything's going to be fine. The season only has a few games left anyway. Next year, Jamie will come back and I'll go back to being a first baseman.* Those positive thoughts were followed by some negative thoughts. *What if I can't throw a strike and I walk like ten batters in a row and Coach pulls me from the game and all my teammates stop liking me and* – I stopped myself in the middle of these jumbled thoughts.

I flipped the light switch on and sat upright in my favorite chair. I squashed my anxiety by turning on the radio and listening to the last few innings of the Arizona Scorpions game. The Scorpions were Arizona's Major League Baseball team and tonight they were facing off with the Detroit Motors.

I was definitely one of the biggest Scorpion fans in Arizona. Although I gave up competing in baseball after just one season, a big part of me was still in love with the sport. Not only did I either watch or listen to nearly every game, I spent hours watching their instructional hitting videos and writing letters to some of my favorite players, like Valentine, Rucker, Reyes and Kraft.

Baseball maintained an important role on the Field, too. My brother Carlos and I spent countless hours living out our fantasy baseball adventures there. We'd pretend to be the Scorpions' all-star pitcher and catcher and set the scene at the World Series, Game 7, sometimes two runners on base, one out, sometimes the bases loaded, two outs. Carlos would crouch down, and with his fingers he'd relay the pitch sign between his legs. Then I'd windup and hurl the overhand pitch to the invisible batter, who always made an out.

Carlos couldn't help giving me a hard time about my new softball career. When we were playing out on the Field, he would constantly throw the ball to me underhand and pretend to scream in a girlish voice. Sometimes I would get defensive and yell back at my brother, "Just because I play softball, doesn't mean that I'm not tough, Carlos. We play just as hard as the boys do." Although I truly believed this statement, my brother's jokes got to me sometimes.

The truth was, although I still loved baseball, softball was becoming a bigger and bigger part of my life. Every day on the softball field I gained more friends and became more of a leader in the lineup. And even though Carlos and Joe made fun of me, no one was happier than Mom. Recognizing my boy-dominated neighborhood, she always wanted me to connect with some girls. Seeing me bring home a softball teammate on the weekends or go to a slumber party really thrilled her.

Mom was easy to spot when she was in the stands at my games. She always sat in her lawn chair up against the backstop fence, shaking her rock-filled soda can loudly. She'd yell and scream and cheer, jumping up and down with every play. It was great, but really embarrassing at the same time. Without fail, during every one of my at bats she'd shake the can and scream something like, "Hit it out of the park, Selena! You can do it!" The vibration of her words in my ears made me feel like she was standing at the plate next to me.

The day after my first experience practicing pitching to Coach in the outfield, Mom was in her chair directly behind home plate. I could hear her all the way from first base when I was in the field and she screamed twice as loud when our team came up to bat. When the time came for me to take the mound in the top of the seventh inning, I thought Mom was going to explode. We were leading 9-5 in the top of the seventh and I guess Coach felt like this was a great chance to get me some much-needed game experience. In Bobby Sox Softball we only played seven innings. This meant that all I had to do was get three outs before our opponent scored four runs, and we'd win the game. Although I was admittedly nervous as I dug my foot into the pitcher's mound, I remembered pitching to Elizabeth before the game. This calmed some of my nerves. To my surprise, I had actually thrown some strikes to her earlier. I only hoped I would be able to do the same thing on the mound when I faced a real batter.

After tossing my final warm up pitch, Elizabeth took the softball and threw it down to second base, signaling the end of our between-innings warm up. Our shortstop, Anne, tossed me the ball and hollered, "Eat 'em up, Superestrella Cinderella!" I had acquired that nickname, which means *Cinderella Superstar* in Spanish, from the fancy bows Mom made for my game day ponytails. I know it sounds corny but I loved the colors Mom would put into my hair. Her ribbons and bows made me feel like I was different than everyone else, like I had something nobody else had.

When I turned toward the plate to start the inning, I noticed the straight-on view I had of my parents. Dad sat on the edge of the bench beside Mom in her lawn chair. Their position behind the backstop soothed my tension. I took a deep breath with my adrenaline pumping. My first pitch flew high and wide, just like the first pitch I threw to Coach Shepard the day before. It hit the backstop with a clank, and I forced a smile, relieving some of my own tension. Elizabeth jumped to her feet to try and make the catch but the ball was well out of her reach, clearing her head by about four feet.

"That's alright, Mi hija!" Mom hollered and shook her can loudly. "Just relax. You can do it!"

Struggling with my footing on the mound, my second pitch landed in the dirt. Ball two. Now I was starting to sweat a little bit and as I glanced over my shoulder and wiped off my sweaty forehead, I could see the body language of my teammates change. Laura Simpson was now holding her hands on her knees at third, our outfielders were kicking at the dirt and Elizabeth was punching the center of her mitt nervously. My lack of confidence and energy on the mound was spreading around the field like a fire. The pressure really mounted when I threw a third straight ball.

This one just missed the strike zone, which was much better than I could say for the first two pitches. Unfortunately, the umpire was unmerciful, resulting in a 3-0 count. Fueled by frustration, my fourth pitch nearly hit the batter and I kicked the dirt as she walked toward first base. I had committed the ultimate pitcher's sin: I'd walked the leadoff batter on four straight pitches to start an inning. Now the girls in the opposing team's dugout started cheering louder. I could barely hear the shaking of Mom's can at this point.

Elizabeth asked the umpire for a time out and she jogged to the mound, her catcher's gear bouncing from side to side. "You didn't hit her, so that was good," Elizabeth needled me with her dry sense of humor, forcing me to laugh and loosen up my shoulders. "You're fine, Selena. Just focus on my glove, and only my glove. You're looking around the field too much, thinking too much. It's just you and me out here, just like before the game. You can do this."

I shook my head slowly, barely listening to her comments. Elizabeth could tell that she wasn't getting through to me. "Do you want to give up, Selena? Because Coach can always put Jessica in and—" My eyes met Elizabeth's and she stopped talking. In the few months Elizabeth had known me, she'd immediately recognized a fire within me similar to her own. She knew I couldn't turn down a challenge. Asking me if I wanted to quit was an easy way to get my full attention.

I squinted my eyes at her, half-scared and half-excited. "Are you kidding me, Elizabeth? Keep Jessica in left field. I'll finish this thing. Just put your glove up and I'll hit it."

Elizabeth smiled. "Good. Now that's the Selena I know."

As the next batter dug in, I concentrated only on Elizabeth's brown catcher's mitt. I ignored Mom and Dad's cheers, my nervous teammates, my noisy opponents, the hot Arizona sun and Coach's habit of running his fingers through his thinning hair. All I saw was the center of Elizabeth's glove. I set my feet, gripped the ball and released the next pitch in one smooth motion. My hand's natural follow through landed my pitch in the heart of the leather glove with a loud pop. Strike one! *How did I do that?* I thought.

Elizabeth flipped off her mask and smiled at me. I couldn't wait to get the ball back from her after that one. I stared at the target again and my next pitch sailed right in line, pop, strike two. Now I was getting into a rhythm. I stared down the batter and tossed another perfect pitch—right down the middle of the plate. This one may have been too perfect because the batter ripped it right back at me. Reacting on pure instincts, I threw my glove in front of my face and snared the bullet. That was a close one.

"One out!" I yelled, holding up my pointer finger to the outfielders, reminding them of the situation. It didn't take long for me to realize that there was more to pitching than simply throwing strikes. I had to be a leader on the field and show a complete sense of control to my teammates and the opposing hitters.

I started off the next batter with another pitch down the middle. That pitch was smacked into the left center field gap for a double, scoring the runner I had previously walked. Knowing we still led 9-6 kept me pretty calm. I had consistently been finding the strike zone and that was a positive. Now I just needed to start moving the ball around the plate a little, maybe changing speeds a bit too. *So how do I do that?* I wondered. I motioned for Elizabeth to visit the mound again.

When she reached me, I placed my glove over my mouth, trying to hide my words by speaking through the leather webbing. "Start moving your glove toward the corners. I think if I focus on it, I can hit some different spots."

Elizabeth smacked me on the back with her glove. "You got it!"

On the next pitch, Elizabeth placed her glove on the inside part of the plate and I hit the corner for strike one. Even though my heart was racing and the stress of being out there in front of everyone was killing me, after that toss, I had officially fallen in love with pitching. I tried not to get too excited on the mound, but the truth was, I had found my calling and I knew it. This time, I aimed for the outside corner on pitch two but missed by a few inches.

Elizabeth switched back to the inside and again I was on target, but the batter managed to make contact with this one. The ball bounced weakly off the handle of the bat and our third baseman, Laura Simpson, ran toward the plate for the barehanded play. She scooped the ball cleanly, but her off-balance throw sailed wide down the first baseline. The runner from second scored on the play, narrowing our lead to 9-7.

Negative thoughts began to spin around in my head like clothes in a washing machine. *How could Laura miss that one? Shoot. If she would have*—I stopped myself, realizing how unfair I was being. I'd made plenty of errors in the field before. For the first time in my short athletic career I understood the magnitude of a fielding error in the eyes of a pitcher. I couldn't blame my teammates—I had to move on. I'd done everything right. My inside pitch had jammed the batter perfectly and her slow roller to third should have been an out. Instead, our lead had been cut to just two runs. None of this mattered though. How I would react to my teammate's error was the only question that I had to answer at this point.

I took a deep breath and pulled my cap down on my head, covering my eyes from the glare of the batter's aluminum bat. Hillary Jax was a friend of mine from school and was a tall, muscular girl with a huge uppercut swing. I'd watched her crush a double earlier in the game off of Marissa. When she stepped to the plate, Elizabeth pointed to the ground and crouched behind her, urging me to keep my pitches low. Hillary lined up very close to the plate with one out and a runner on second. She looked intimidating and reality started to set in. We had outplayed this team for the entire game and I was about to blow it in the last inning.

I managed to work the count to one ball and two strikes on three decent pitches. Using a stronger leg push off the rubber, I actually threw my fourth pitch really fast. Hillary was surprised and had a hard time catching up with my fastball, bouncing it softly to first base for the second out. *That was a good pitch*, I thought.

Now I needed just one more out to classify my pitching debut as a success. With a runner on second, the cleanup hitter came to the plate and glared at me confidently. My first three pitches were low and hard, producing a 2-1 count. The adrenaline pumping through my body combined with my new leg push had me throwing much harder than I had earlier in the inning. The next pitch elevated coming off my hand and reached the batter right about chest high. She took a hefty swing at this one, sending the ball high to short left field. I pointed up in the air immediately as I watched the ball soar toward Jessica McDonald, who ran under it quickly and seemed to have it tracked. Jessica was a great fielder and I sighed with relief, knowing that the game was about to be over. But as the ball came down, Jessica lost it in the bright sun. She allowed it to drop in front of her untouched. The runner from second base scored and our lead was cut to just one run.

I tugged on my hat again as I headed back to the mound. My stomach muscles tightened and I bent down to retie the lace on my right cleat. This was a stall tactic I had learned from watching Scorpions pitchers, who used this routine often when they got into a jam. I looked up a few seconds later and glanced over to the dugout at Coach Shepard. He nodded his head and clapped his hands encouragingly. I nodded back at him in affirmation, trying hard not to let my body betray me by showing Coach how nervous I was. My hands were shaking. Sweat was dripping down my back. I could actually hear my heart beating over the loud shaking of Mom's soda can and all the sounds of a potential come-from-behind win.

As my toes settled on the rubber I zoned in on the plate. Elizabeth pounded her glove enthusiastically. "Right here, Selena! Right here!"

Dad's words of encouragement were clear in the chaos of the moment. "Just one more out, Selena!"

On the first pitch I hit the outside corner, leaving the batter baffled for strike one. That was just where I'd aimed it. Feeling confident, I tried the same spot again, but missed low. The stray pitch evened the count at one and one. Elizabeth slid inside on the next pitch and with a smooth windmill rotation I connected with her glove. Pop! Strike two! The crowd stood on their feet. I was so pumped up by the moment that I tried to push off the rubber extra hard on the next few pitches and ended up losing my control. Before I knew it, the count was full, three balls and two strikes.

With a runner on second, two outs, and our team leading 9-8, I took another deep breath and approached the mound. Elizabeth positioned her glove a bit inside again, a spot I had been hitting with some degree of consistency. As I released the ball, it headed in that direction, but the batter swung quickly and smashed a line drive.

If it stayed fair, the game would be tied. *Go foul, go foul, go foul.* I leaned toward the line, trying to urge the ball. Luckily, the ball landed just past the white line in left field. "Foul ball," the umpire shouted. *That was a close one,* I thought.

I turned my back to the plate and smirked in relief at my teammates. Our shortstop, Anne Fishburn, smiled back at me. "Finish her off, Superestrella Cinderella!" she shouted.

I took my glove off behind the mound and rubbed the ball in the palm of my hands, squeezing as hard as I could to relieve my nervousness. A crazy idea entered my head. The batter was swinging way out in front of my pitches. It was a perfect time to throw my very first changeup. A changeup is thrown with the same windmill arm speed as a fastball, but the ball floats out of the pitcher's hand much slower than a fastball, fooling the batter. In warm-ups before the game, Elizabeth showed me how to throw "the change" by cupping my fingers around the ball and burying it in the palm of my hand. With small hands and even smaller fingers, I found this grip to be no easy task. But wanting to secure the win and knowing that the batter was ahead of my fastball, I was willing to risk everything on the next pitch.

I reached down, scooping up a pile of dirt in my right hand and letting it run through my fingers smoothly. Sticking my hand into my glove, I used the friction of the sand to stretch my fingers and palm around the ball. I concentrated on Elizabeth's glove and repeated the same fast windmill motion that had become natural for me that day. Just as my hand released the ball, I watched it float in slow motion toward home plate. Everyone was surprised by my trick pitch, particularly the batter. She had timed her swing for a fastball and took a huge cut way out in front of my final pitch. The ball landed softly in the middle of Elizabeth's glove and the umpire shouted the sweetest words ever—"Strike three! That's the ball game!"

I pounded my fist into my glove in excitement. I did it! It wasn't pretty, but we'd won the game. My teammates rushed around me, offering hugs, knuckle bumps and high fives. Coach Shepard joined our celebration. "Looks like we've got a new pitcher, girls!" he smiled.

I felt like I was glowing as I soaked up the amazing moment. Although I still loved first base, I knew that I wanted to be a full-time pitcher. With one stressful save under my belt and a great group of friends to lean on, life couldn't have been going better.

CHAPTER FOUR

A GOODNIGHT KISS

"Come on guys, dinner's ready!" Mom yelled the familiar phrase from the kitchen, her favorite room in our apartment. The boys turned off their video games and Dad stopped reading his magazine as they all raced down the hallway, bumping into each other playfully on their way. I finished helping Mom set the table by dropping three ice cubes into everyone's glass.

We'd returned home from the first softball game I'd ever pitched an hour earlier and I was still floating from the excitement. I paced around the kitchen as Mom pulled one of her homemade specialties out of the oven. Just smelling Mom's cooking made me hungry. She had cooked her famous hot tamales with her awesome refried beans and rice. Mom cooked traditional Mexican food every chance she got. She thought it was important for us to stay close to our roots. It was a great way to keep us connected to the Mexican culture was through Mom's cooking. She and Dad also spoke to each other in Spanish often, and Mom sung Spanish songs around the house all the time. My brothers and I spoke both English and Spanish because of the frequency both languages were used around our house.

The whole family gathered around our old wood dining table anxiously eyeing the tamales and fresh corn tortillas. The chewed up corners of the wood table, courtesy of our dog, Campeona, were hidden by a bright yellow tablecloth Mom had sewn herself two summers ago. The embroidery surrounding the edges was made to look identical to the tablecloth Mom had grown up with as a child in Tijuana, a city in Northern Mexico. My grandmother had sewn her family the original version of our yellow tablecloth nearly fifty years earlier! We couldn't afford to buy a new table after Campeona used the corners of this one as a chew toy. So instead, Mom bought some fabric and went to work—a perfect example of her tremendous spirit.

"When you get lemons, you make lemonade." Mom would always use that expression to my brothers and me. We were never exactly sure what she meant by that, but I think it had something to do with doing the best you could with what you were given. This was always Mom's attitude. So even when times were tough, our family remained positive. She had a way of making the darkness turn to light and the sour turn into sweetness for all of us.

Everyone sat down in their regular seats as Mom covered the table with mounds of food. As usual, I sat between Joe and Carlos, a custom Dad started a few years earlier in order to separate the boys, who were always poking at each other or kicking one another under the table. Although my tiny body did a decent job of separating them, it wasn't uncommon for me to receive an occasional shoe to the shin during a meal. Not today, though. When hot tamales and corn tortillas were on the table, the boys were

38

almost always silent, aside from the occasional request for more salsa.

"So boys, did you hear about Selena's big game?" Mom spoke to my brothers, whose focus was barely interrupted as they piled refried beans into their tortillas.

"Yeah, Dad told us all about it," said Joe, revealing his lack of interest through the drone in his voice.

"She was awesome!" Dad echoed Mom's excitement, looking over at me and raising his eyebrows.

"How awesome can you be at *soft*ball?" Joe laughed, heavily accenting the word soft. My heart sank for a moment, but when Joe looked over at me and saw that his comment had really hurt my feelings, he changed his tone. "Jeez, I'm only kidding, Selena. I know how good you are."

I started to speak quickly in response to my brother's slight acknowledgement of my talent. "Only one batter really hit the ball hard and I caught it, Joe." My focus quickly turned away from Joe on my left and toward Carlos on my right. "Carlos, remember how you told me about the first time you pitched? How you said that you loved being in control of the game. Remember? Well, me too. It was just like that for me. I loved being on the mound. I mean, I know my teammates helped me in the field, but I still had to get the ball over the plate. I still had to look all those batters right in their eyes before I threw a pitch to them." I smiled, and then got serious, showing the boys exactly how I stared down the hitters I faced.

Dad nodded, finishing his bite before responding. "Aside from the first batter, you didn't have any problems throwing strikes." He nudged Joe. "Your sister is really something, Jose." Dad always came to my rescue. I was his baby girl and he was very protective of me. Dinner went on like that for the next fifteen minutes or so. I recapped nearly every pitch and every feeling that went through my head and body during that game. Mom smiled, Dad nodded and my brothers gobbled tamale after tamale.

I jumped into a hot shower right after dinner, unable to get the feeling of excitement out of my head. When the spraying water drowned out all the other sounds in the house I began to daydream about pitching in middle school, in high school, in college, in the Olympics—and then—"Hurry up, Selena!" I heard Carlos pounding on the locked door. In an apartment with only one bathroom, there is just enough time to brush your teeth, and use the bathroom and shower—daydreaming was a luxury we couldn't afford.

Ten minutes later, after drying off and putting on the pajamas that my aunt had bought for me last year, I ran over to Mom, sitting on the foot of her bed. Dad and the boys were watching television, which was pretty much what they did together every night after my brothers had finished their homework. Mom lay down next to me on the bed, totally exhausted. She sighed heavily and closed her eyes for a moment. She had worked a nine-hour day, then cheered louder than anyone for two hours during my softball game. Right after that, she came home and cooked and cleaned dinner for five! And I thought I was tired from school and softball.

She ran her fingers through my hair gently. "What do you think about curls for tomorrow's dance, Mi hija?" Tomorrow was Friday and it was the father-daughter dance at my school, La Presa Elementary.

"Sure," I answered. "If you're tired, though, I can just—"

"Shhhhh," she sat up and began combing out my hair, wrapping my long, black locks in huge curlers that she had forced Joe to bring to us from under the bathroom sink. We both laughed as he searched aimlessly through the mess of hair products.

Mom worked quickly, humming softly as she carefully placed my hair in the curlers. Before I even got the chance to take a look at myself, Mom told me that the curlers looked like a bunch of toilet paper rolls stuck to my head. I laughed again as I rushed toward the mirror to see myself. Knowing I had to sleep in the curlers, I tested them out right away, lying down on Mom's bed. The discomfort caused me to sit up immediately. "How do I sleep like this?" I asked.

Mom shrugged her shoulders. "You'll manage."

Sometimes I felt really unlucky to be a girl. I mean, it was so easy for the boys, with their short hair and dirty fingernails. Especially when it came to sports. I was always good at sports, but because I was a girl, everyone expected me to prefer dolls to baseball gloves. But I didn't. Sure, I liked to wear nice clothes and it felt great when people said that I had a pretty face. But still, compared to getting ready to play ball it was a lot of work getting a girl like me ready for a dance. I touched the rollers on my head again as I sneaked a peek in the living room, where my lazy brothers were comfortably sprawled out on our old tan couch, which doubled as my bed. "Oh well," I sighed. "I won't sleep much, but at least I'll look pretty for the dance."

Mom laughed at this comment. "You'll sleep fine. It just feels a little funny at first."

"It feels like I have a pile of bricks sticking into the back of my head. How am I supposed to sleep with a brick head?"

Mom laughed again, this time much harder. "You can take my special pillow with you to bed tonight, Mi hija. That should help

41

with the bricks." She left the room for a minute and returned with a shiny, rose-colored dress, which was accented with a large bow in the back. She was also carrying her special pillow. "I ironed your dress," she handed it to me and I thanked her. Then she handed me her special pillow from off of her bed. "This, though, I want back tomorrow night." She playfully tossed the pillow at my face, but as she followed through with the throwing motion, she grimaced and started rubbing her chest with her right hand just below her left shoulder.

"Are you alright Mom?" I placed the pillow back on the bed.

"Just a little heartburn from dinner. I'm fine. I'm just glad you're out there pitching and not me."

Dad chimed in sarcastically from the other room. "Heartburn, Maria? From tamales and refried beans? No!" Dad was making a rare attempt at a joke. Mom's cooking was delicious, but some traditional Mexican cuisine was rough on the stomach.

Mom sat down again as I tried on my dress for her. I did a silly imitation of a ballerina, prancing in circles around the room with my curlers bouncing all over the place. I even tried spinning on my toe, but tripped in the process. I had never been graceful, which was why I preferred softball to dancing. Mom and I laughed uncontrollably as she twirled me around like her dance partner. She was equally ungraceful, but her beautiful voice made up for it as she started to sing. We twirled and twirled around the room together until we were dizzy.

Knowing it was late, Mom held my hand and walked me to the old, tan corduroy couch. "Okay boys, off your sister's bed." She smacked my brothers playfully on the backs of their heads and they quickly scattered into their shared bedroom after kissing Mom on the cheek. Then Mom laid me down, wrapping my warm blanket around me as she squeezed me tight and kissed me on the forehead.

"What a great day." Her smile was big and bright.

I answered back, "Yeah, I think I'm gonna always pitch from now on. If they'll let me, that is."

Mom smiled. "They'll let you. You were great and you really seemed to love it out there."

"I did." I smiled thinking about the feeling I had on the mound that day, the feeling of belonging, of finding my calling. "I love you, Mom."

"I love you too, Selena." She kissed me again on the forehead and shut the lamp off near my head.

As she turned the corner into her room, I felt drawn to call her back. "Hey Mom." She returned to my side again. "Are you sure you're okay?" I asked.

"Yes, I'm just really tired." A long hard day like this one was not unusual for my mother. Being exhausted made sense to me. I was tired just thinking about all she had done today.

"Well, thanks for coming to my game and for getting me ready for the dance."

Staring at me with her warm, brown eyes, she paused a moment before kissing me on the forehead. "Sweet dreams, Mi hija." I slept soundly that night, dreaming of stepping onto that pitcher's mound again.

The next morning I awoke early to the horrible sound of weeping.

That morning my entire life changed. I ripped off the blankets immediately upon waking, and ran down the hall as fast as I could. When I reached my parents' bedroom, I found Dad sitting in his bed, crying uncontrollably. Mom's body was lying limp in his arms as he looked toward the ceiling and cried.

I stood in the doorway with my brothers behind me, frozen in shock. Tears welled up in my eyes as I waited for Mom to wake up. She never did. I don't remember much about the rest of that day, only that I had never seen my father look so scared or so sad. In my short ten years of life, I'd experienced different kinds of loss. I'd lost countless baseball games on the Field, I lost to Dad nearly every time we played chess against one another, and one time I lost a math assignment that took me over five hours to finish. Nothing could have prepared me for the loss I encountered on June 15, when my mother, Maria Nora Garcia, passed away in her sleep.

Death had come into my house and life would never be the same for me. Never before had I understood death's deep darkness. Never before had I felt the pain myself or understood the permanency of it.

As I sat staring at the casket during my mother's funeral, I held her prayer card in both my hands. On the prayer card was a simple picture of her radiant, smiling face, shiny black hair and warm brown eyes. It brought back memories—memories of Mom's one and only hitting appearance on the Field, of her singing while she brushed my hair, of her can-shaking cheers at my softball games, and of course, of our final moments together, dancing, laughing and then kissing each other goodnight.

I didn't hear anything that was said that day at the funeral. I didn't feel any of the hugs or handshakes. I felt numb, lifeless, dried up, empty. Like a fish in the desert.

I missed fifth grade graduation and all the festivities that went with it—including the father-daughter dance. I didn't care about any of that stuff with Mom gone. In fact, I wondered if I would ever want to dance again. My eleventh birthday was the quietest of my life. I didn't even eat a piece of the cake Dad bought for me. I also quit playing softball and spent most of my summer days staring blankly at the walls, the tablecloth that Mom had made, and everything else in the apartment that reminded me of her absence.

Three months later, even entering middle school didn't excite me. School became like a job that I hated. I'd arrive in the morning, do the bare minimum, and then go home in the afternoon to the sadness of our empty apartment. With Mom gone, I didn't know what I wanted to do with my life. Nothing seemed important to me anymore.

CHAPTER FIVE

A CHALLENGE

My transition into middle school was absolutely horrible. In the year after Mom's death, I became a recluse. I rarely left our apartment, and the only person I really spoke to was my brother, Carlos. Joe was in high school and although we saw each other a lot, he was very wrapped up in his own world. It seemed like no one understood the agony I felt inside. Sure, my brothers experienced the same painful loss that I did, but they never really talked about it. In fact, they seemed to be able to go about their lives almost like normal, hanging out with their friends, playing sports and going to school. I knew they missed Mom too, but it was so much harder for me.

Every day when Carlos and I walked through the front door to our empty apartment after school, he would drop his backpack and head across the street to the Field. There, all of his problems disappeared for a few hours. Although he was nice enough to invite me, I had no interest in stepping foot on our neighborhood turf. I'd quit playing sports after Mom's death and I planned to stay away from participating in them forever. I still watched the Scorpions play on television almost every night, though. It was one of the few things Dad and I did together and it really made me feel better. Aside from television, I was completely disconnected with baseball and softball.

Near the end of my sixth grade school year something finally happened that helped me out of my funk. It all started when Carlos and I dropped by the library after school to check out some books for a history report. As we walked by the librarian, Mrs. Englewood, we noticed a large, cardboard poster publicizing a "Readathon Challenge." A picture of Arizona Scorpions home-run-hitting king, Jose Valentine, was attached to the side.

As we passed by, I didn't even take the time to read the details, but Carlos stalled excitedly at the desk. He eventually caught up to me in the back of the library and playfully slapped me on the shoulder. "Hey, Selena, did you see that Readathon sign? Did you see the prizes?"

Carlos held a neon yellow flyer in his hand, running his finger straight down to the prize category. He read aloud: "There are first, second and third place prizes for each grade level, plus a grand prize!" His eyes opened wide as he spoke. "Third place prizes are five dollar gift-certificates for ice cream. Second place prizes are movie tickets. First place prizes are two tickets to an Arizona Scorpions baseball game. And the grand prize, for the student who reads the most books in the entire school, is two tickets to an Arizona Scorpions game **PLUS** a personal tour of Arizona Stadium during batting practice." I raised my head from my book as Carlos slapped me on the back again. He could hardly maintain his hushed library voice. "Can you imagine, Selena? Batting practice with the Scorpions!"

I tried to turn my focus back to the bookcase and pretend I wasn't interested. "Thanks Carlos, but no thanks."

Carlos was well aware of my mental state since Mom's death, and he simply would not give up. "Come on, Selena! Imagine being on the field with Jose Valentine and Tony Rocker. Would that be awesome or what?"

I quickly put my hand over his mouth, trying to muffle his excitement. "Shhh, we're in the library."

Carlos tried his best to lower his voice. "Well, I bet I can read more books than you can, anyway."

He was trying to get into my head, knowing that I hated turning down a challenge. "That doesn't work on me anymore, Carlos," I calmly explained to my brother.

He paused for a second as I flipped through a history book about the American Civil War, the reason we'd stopped by the library in the first place. For some reason, he desperately wanted me to enter this contest. But I wasn't budging. That is, until he said something that really made my blood start to boil, "What would Mom think of the way you're acting, Selena?"

His words echoed in my ears and I nearly dropped the book I was flipping through. The truth was, I knew exactly what Mom would think. She would want me to stop feeling sorry for myself, to start improving my grades, to join the softball team again, to start wearing ribbons and bows in my hair again, and most of all, to bring the smile back to my face. Although I knew this, it was still hard to accept. "Mom is dead, Carlos," I replied coldly to his comment and started to walk away, near tears.

Immediately, my brother grabbed me by the arm and spoke

more forcefully. "Wait a minute! I loved Mom too, Selena. And *I* still remember how she wanted us to do great things in our lives. Maybe you forgot." He paused, his tone softening, "Do you remember what she used to say to us? When you get lemons—"

"You make lemonade," I finished his sentence and our eyes met as a tear ran down my cheek.

Carlos gave me a hug and I started to cry for a second, thinking about Mom and how I had been letting her down lately. After a few moments in deep thought, I spoke through my tears. "You're right. I'll do it Carlos." We reached out our right hands and knocked fists, sealing the pact.

Ten minutes later I had loaded five sports books into my arms and was genuinely excited to get started with the contest. I picked up a fictional story about a baseball player heading to the majors and a softball instructional book focusing on pitching. I also picked up a book about basketball legend Larry Hawk, one on football great Julius Lucas and an autobiography written by soccer standout Maria Cooper. I would have heaped my stack solely with baseball and softball, but I knew mixing in a few other sports would help me avoid burning out too quickly.

The Readathon Challenge had my competitive juices flowing. I read all five of those books cover to cover and returned three days later to check out five more. I could feel the competition nipping at my heels and was propelled to read more and more books. For the first time in a long time I felt my adrenaline pumping the way I used to when I was out on the diamond. Plus, the stories of the sports heroes I was reading about within the pages of the books really interested me. I learned all kinds of cool stuff. Like how All-American swimming sensation, Carl Stokes, ate graham crackers and milk before every meet. I loved the superstitions of Olympic softball player Sheila Mitchell, who wore black and white striped wristbands every time she came to bat in a slump. She said the black and white wristbands helped her to "…break out of jail." Once again, the joy of sports was running through my veins, even though I was not physically participating in them.

For the next four weeks, my after-school activities included only two things: homework and reading. My persistence allowed me to walk through the Highlands Middle School library door on May 2 with my log sheet jammed from top to bottom with the thirty-four books that I'd read. Plus, each book required a paragraph summary, so my log sheet was about ten pages long! I smiled confidently as I handed off the stack of papers to Mrs. Englewood. My sidekick, Carlos, who was competing for the eighth grade, did the same, although his thirteen-book effort came up well short of mine.

The next twenty-four hours were a slow torment. But the feeling radically reversed once Carlos and I sat down in the school auditorium the next afternoon. Our school principal, Mrs. Julian, stepped to the podium holding a single sheet of paper in her hand. At first, she talked about the school play that was starting next week and then she went on to congratulate our cheerleading team for their second-place finish at a statewide meet last week. I nervously rubbed my thumbs together as I waited for her to finally cut to the chase. I slid to the edge of my seat after she mentioned the contest. Sixth grade was going to be the first class to receive awards and before I knew it, she said, "The winner for sixth grade is Selena Garcia!"

I started tapping my feet in excitement and relief, knowing

that winning my grade guaranteed me two tickets to the Scorpions game. But the real question was whether or not I was the best in the school. That's what counted—that's what would get me the tour of the stadium and an opportunity to step onto a professional field. I reeled in my emotions quickly, realizing that seventh and eighth grade still needed to be announced. "The first place winner for seventh grade is Nathan Jaybee!"

I dropped my head into my hands. Only one more grade to go. "And the first-place winner for eighth grade is Hanna Mendoza!" Before another thought could pop into my head, Mrs. Julian trumpeted loudly, "And the grand prize winner of the Readathon Challenge, the person who read the most books in all of Highlands Middle School is Selena Garcia from the sixth grade with thirty four books!"

Cheers and claps surrounded me as I jumped up from my seat. I used Carlos as my springboard, pushing off his knees to enter the middle row. As I headed down the aisle to accept my certificate, my feet shuffled at the pace of a home run trot, fast enough to admit excitement, but slow enough to appreciate the moment.

When I returned to my seat I was holding an envelope with two tickets and a certificate of achievement. I gave my brother a tight hug. "We're going, man! We're gonna see the Scorpions up close and personal!" I looked up at the ceiling and wondered if Mom was watching me at that moment. I was sure that she'd be proud if she was. For the first time since her death, I felt my heart thump with excitement. It seemed strange to feel warmth in my cheeks again, but I actually had something to smile about in my life.

The Scorpions game was four weeks later and I couldn't

have been more excited. That day at school was kind of a waste for me. The good news was that in the last month or so, I had gotten back to being a good student. With some hard work, I had raised my average up to a solid B. Still, on this day, all I could think about was the ring of the final bell. Making my way to Arizona Stadium was the only thing on my mind.

Just minutes after Carlos and I arrived home from school, we jumped into Dad's pickup and headed to the ballpark. The drive from our town of Tierra de Sueño to Arizona Stadium took about two hours. But the time flew by as Carlos and I tried to predict all that would go on during our visit to the Scorpions' royal residence. Dad's only interruption came as we reached the "Scorpion Way" exit and the awesome site of Arizona Stadium came within full view. "There it is guys!" He pointed to the huge building on the right hand side of the car. Carlos and I immediately slid over to the window.

"No way!" I turned and knuckle bumped Carlos.

In my eleven years of life, I had never stepped into a professional baseball stadium. Today was not only going to be my first trip to a real live pro baseball game, but I was actually going to get a chance to stand on the field!

Dad purchased a ticket for himself and Carlos and I entered the game with the two free tickets I had won. Our seats were in a great location, directly above the Scorpions dugout. After checking me into the public relations office, Dad and Carlos found their seats.

A short, older lady with thick rim glasses offered her right hand to me, which I shook with a firm grip. "I'm Pat Rogers, I'll be giving you the tour of the stadium. You must be Selena." We shook hands and I smiled nervously. "Well, here's your field pass, Selena, just make sure you keep it around your neck at all times. We'll be leaving in a few minutes, we just have to wait for two more students to arrive." The Readathon Challenge was offered throughout the Tierra de Sueño school district and one student from each of the twelve middle schools in the area earned the grand prize. As I finished flipping through the pages of the slick, colorful Scorpions program that Pat had given to me, the last two students reached the office. Finally the excursion I had dreamed about for so many nights was under way.

As our group of eight boys and four girls stepped into the elevator, I shuffled my way into the back corner. Scrunched against the wall, I looked up above the door and watched the lit floor numbers decrease. My heart pounded in anticipation. When the elevator doors opened I realized where I was: beneath the stadium, a place I had never dreamed of seeing in person.

We approached the locker-room door and my senses immediately heightened. My nose flared as the sharp odor of muscle ointment filled the air. My ears perked up at the sound of music blaring from the four stereo speakers, which hung in the corners of the room. Strolling by the lockers, my eyes widened as I read the names on the gold plaques located above the wood stalls: #31 Jose Valentine, #19 Tony Rocker, #14 Dan Foote, #51 Trevor Kraft. Glistening white jerseys with players' names sewn in blue letters hung in each locker. Gloves, boxes of cleats and dozens of bats filled the open spaces. Some players, like Tony Rocker, decorated their lockers with pictures of family or pretty girls. I reached down and touched the carpet without anyone noticing. I rubbed my fingers through the plush Scorpions logo, which was embedded in the middle of the floor. There was no doubt that this was the coolest room I had ever seen.

As we headed out of the clubhouse I turned around for one last glimpse. Then I turned toward the hallway and noticed our group heading down a long tunnel. This tunnel was dimly lit and shaped like an upside-down U. The walls were covered with photographs of past Scorpion players in action. I jogged to catch up with the rest of the group, making sure to take a quick look at each picture on my way. As I moved toward the end of the corridor, a light glistened in the distance, causing me to close my eyes abruptly. Within twenty seconds I stood at the bottom of the tunnel, leading to the vast openness of the field—like a stem supporting a fully blossomed flower. The massive concrete ring of the stadium cradled the velvet green grass, and the banks of lights from above shone down on the red brick clay. I took my first steps onto the field and felt the excitement running through my veins. My eyes were wider than ever before as I whispered to myself, *"whoa."*

I was out of my trance a moment later when I heard the sweet sound of wood connecting with the leather of a tightly wound baseball. My attention quickly turned toward the batting cage. "Crack!" "Crack!" "Crack!" The Scorpions had just begun batting practice and a group of players were taking turns in the cage. I sat down on the bench inside the dugout and instantaneously sunk into the cushion-lined seat. *This is so cool,* I thought. Leaning back, I slowly swung my legs, which were too short to touch the rubber mats below. As I looked down both sides of the bench, I imagined all the strategy and baseball talk that occurred during a game in this very dugout. I had to smile.

Just then I noticed Jose Valentine stepping to the plate. I

stood and walked over to the grass edging, admiring the giant body and thick muscles of the home run-hitting machine. His quick bat speed produced a line drive into the gap, a blast over the left field wall, a one-hopper over third base, a grounder up the middle and then a shot over the right-center field wall. *Five-for-five*, I thought.

Several other Scorpions took their turns in the batting cage, each switching off after five pitches. Groups of position players moved from fielding, to running the base paths, to batting, while most of the pitchers ran and stretched in the outfield. The pregame warm-up worked like the internal mechanism of a clock—one gear moving another gear, which moved another gear. The players' foot quickness while fielding balls, the laser speed of their throws and the explosive power of their bats overwhelmed me. But nothing stunned me more than the physical presence of the 6-foot-5-inch, 250-pound Valentine, who walked over to our group after batting practice. "How you guys doing?" He stuck out his gigantic hand to each of us.

Looking up at his goatee-accented face, I smiled, as my dinky hand was swallowed up by his enormous grip. Valentine grabbed his dark brown bat with his left hand and held it across his chest. "I hear you guys are pretty good readers. Well, I've got another contest for you. I'm going to pick a number between one and one hundred, and whoever gets the closest to the number can have this bat *and* my batting gloves."

Number thirty-one immediately flashed into my mind. That was Valentine's jersey number. I put my hands behind my back, tensely squeezing them together. I could only hope the other students in front of me would avoid my number.

Valentine stared to the sky, thinking of his pick, then lowered his head. "Okay, I got it. Go ahead. We'll start right here." He pointed his finger at the tall, blond girl who stood to the farthest right of the group.

"Fourteen," she responded. And the rest of the kids followed. "Fifty, sixty-one, twenty-three, seventy-nine, forty-two, eight." When it was my turn I released my white-knuckled hands from behind my back and rested them at my sides. I looked upward into Valentine's eyes and confidently declared, "Thirty-one."

After the rest of the kids had guessed their numbers, Valentine lifted up the giant bat, holding it with both hands in the same manner as an auctioneer. "And the winner is," he paused to add some drama, "number," then he pointed to his jersey, "thirty-one!" I lunged toward Valentine, my excitement pushing me forward as I stretched out my hands like a first baseman.

After handing me his bat and his gloves, Valentine stayed around long enough to sign autographs and take a few pictures. Even though I already had Valentine's autograph engraved in the barrel of his bat, I asked him to sign a piece of notebook paper, which I folded up in my pocket for Carlos. After all, if it wasn't for my brother's encouragement, I would never have gotten here.

"So do you play ball?" Valentine asked as he scribbled his name on the lined paper.

I looked away, not wanting to get too sentimental. "Yeah, I used to play softball."

"Used to?" he asked. "You retired already?" He laughed at his own joke.

"No." I forced a smile. "My Mom died a year ago, so I quit playing." I tried hard not to cry as I spoke these words to my hero.

Valentine rested his huge hand softly on my bony shoulder. "I'm sorry to hear that." Wanting to break the uncomfortable silence he continued, "Did she come to a lot of your games?"

"Every single one." I answered.

"Wow, she must have loved watching you, huh?"

"Yeah," I spoke through a tight smile. "And I loved it, too. Especially pitching, but I only got to pitch once." Tears welled up in my eyes again as I began to remember that long day. The day that I fell in love with pitching and lost my best friend.

"I bet you were pretty good with those big biceps of yours." Valentine jokingly pinched my small arm muscle with his monstrous two fingers. It made me laugh as I wiped away a tear from my eye. "I know it's none of my business, but I think your mom would have wanted you to keep playing. Don't you?"

I shyly shook my head. "Yeah, that's what everyone keeps telling me."

"Maybe they're right. Do you think you can find your mitt and get back on a team? You already got some new batting gloves." He paused, waiting for my response. As I shrugged my shoulders in uncertainty, he continued. "I don't know you, but you got here, somehow. And that took heart. I believe you have the heart to get back on the softball field too."

"Thank you, Jose." In that moment, everything kind of stopped. I was standing in Arizona Stadium chatting with Jose Valentine. Talk about a strange moment. All of a sudden I started to smile as I spoke. "I guess you're right, Jose, I really *should* play again."

Valentine offered his hand and we shook on the deal. When we released our grip, I felt as if a huge weight had been lifted off my shoulders. Jose made his way back to his teammates and I made my way into the stands. Just eight rows back from the rail, Dad and Carlos stood, waving and hollering as if I were a rock star. I held up my new bat over my head like a prizefighter holding up his championship belt in the ring. I hugged Dad and his eyes glimmered as he admired the bat I held at my chest. "You deserve this, Selena."

I told Dad and Carlos about my deal with Jose Valentine. As soon as we got back home, I would start my softball career again. I was determined to not only return to the diamond, but to come back as a pitcher.

In between the Scorpions' home runs, strikeouts, and the seventh-inning stretch, I paused to soak in my first great day in a long time. Although I still thought about Mom nearly every hour of every day—especially that night—I could feel the hard shell I'd been hauling around in my mother's absence beginning to crack. I was finally ready to open my wings again and revisit the wonderful world of softball.

CHAPTER SIX

NOBODY'S PERFECT

I knew that attempting to make my comeback as a softball pitcher was going to be extra difficult without a catcher. My brothers were hardly ever around so I had to be creative. Within a few weeks, I discovered the perfect partner just twenty minutes walking distance from our apartment: the old racquetball court at Highlands Middle School.

Every day I made the trip with five softballs, a bottle of water, my glove, and two pieces of white chalk all stuffed in my beat-up duffel bag. A concrete wall intended for racquetball stood about twenty feet high in the middle of the blacktop area. I would draw a square representing the strike zone on the middle portion of the cement structure. Beside the box would be a stick figure batter, on the right side one day and on the left the next. After walking thirty-five steps from the wall, I'd use my chalk to mark a pitching mound on the pavement. Then I'd fire away, wind-milling pitch after pitch after pitch.

Without any distractions I concentrated on changing speeds,

perfecting my changeup and nailing the edges, sending puffs of chalk into the air with each pitch. My control was certainly improving, but I also noticed a major increase in speed as my right arm grew stronger from the practice. I would often use such force on my pitches that the ball would leave a skid mark on the gray stone surface.

My new teammate was special for another reason, too. After riffling a pitch at the wall, I was forced to react and field the ricocheted ball. If I didn't, I'd have to stop my workout every few pitches to pick up all the stray softballs. This system of pitching and fielding helped me to keep my glove work sharp while maintaining a continuous pitching routine. I also started to spend time tossing up balls and hitting them at the wall. And I relived over and over again the funny incidents and special memories I'd made with my teammates on the Orange Crush. Getting back into the game felt great. The drops of sweat that rolled down my forehead really pumped me up. After an hour or so of exercise, I wanted more than anything to play in an actual game again.

Two months after I began my training I was ready for the real thing. I could hardly sit still on the drive over to that first practice. I was really nervous about seeing all my teammates again. *What if they didn't want me back? What if they were upset that I'd quit on them?* These negative thoughts quickly vanished as the entire group of girls greeted me with a giant hug in the parking lot right when Dad dropped me off. *What a relief!*

On the field, I had very little trouble. I slipped right back into the routine, displaying sharp glove work and field awareness. Everyone knew me as a productive fielder and hitter, so they weren't too surprised. But when I hopped onto the mound, my powerful pitching shocked everyone—especially Coach Larry. Throwing off a real mound to my old catcher Elizabeth Lee, I found myself pitching with greater velocity and accuracy than ever before. I threw about ten fastballs in a row that smacked the center of Elizabeth's glove. My teammates circled around me at the mound, their mouths open in shock.

Oddly, the only uncomfortable feeling I experienced that day came from my long black hair, which blew freely in the breeze. With Mom not around, ponytails and braids were out of the question. The ribbons and bows were gone too, as they reminded me of the time we used to spend together each night, and how it was gone forever. My teammates no longer called me by my nickname—Cinderella Superestrella—since my fancy hair bows were gone.

Even so, my heart jumped excitedly thinking about putting on my Orange Crush uniform again. And when our first game arrived, Coach Larry shocked me with an extra special assignment—starting pitcher. Before stepping onto the mound to face the Blue Bombers for my comeback performance, I reached into the back pocket of my shorts and felt Mom's prayer card from her funeral. I vowed to place the photograph there during every game I ever played in. Even though I couldn't see her sitting in her lawn chair behind the backstop, or hear her noisy can shaker, I kept her spirit alive in my heart, in my mind, and in my back pocket.

I anchored my cleats on the freshly dusted rubber and eyed Elizabeth's glove in the center of her chest. Her target seemed to be much bigger than the small strike zone box I used to mark the cement wall. That's when I started to notice that something inside me felt different today. My mind was totally focused on pitching this game. It was as if *this* game was the only thing happening in the entire world, and all the energy within me was aimed at winning it. I began to notice things I had never seen on the mound before. The curves and creases of Elizabeth's mitt became clear to me. I could even see her fingers moving slightly inside of the mitt, behind the thick leather. She was adjusting her target to the exact spot where she wanted my pitch. And somehow, today, I knew I would hit that spot. My arm was powerful and precise, like the arm of a futuristic robot.

After a deep breath and a final hard glance into the eyes of the hitter I twirled my arm forward. The ball zipped out of my hand and snapped the center of Elizabeth's glove like a bee zooming toward the center of a flower. Strike one. The Orange Crush fans erupted in excitement, especially Dad, who sat at the top of the bleachers.

My next two pitches were exact replicas of the first, leaving the Blue Bombers leadoff batter standing motionless as the umpire rung her up for the first out of the game. My heart pattered in excitement at my first success, but my competitive nature quickly sent me back into game mode.

The second Blue Bombers batter dug in and swung at my first offering, an outside pitch that she weakly grounded into Meredith Manning's glove at second. "Great play, Mer." I yelled over to my teammate.

Anxious to ring up the third out, I rushed to the mound and hurried my first pitch. The softball left my hand awkwardly and bounced into the dirt for ball one. I repeated the error on the second pitch, finding myself in a 2-0 hole. Elizabeth flipped off her mask and winked at me, placing her glove in the heart of the plate, then punching the center of her mitt loudly so I could hear it pop. Elizabeth was a great catcher. She knew that I had gotten out of my rhythm and needed to be refocused. Her 'pop' had awoken my senses. I winked back at Elizabeth.

My next pitch was right on target for a strike. The count was now 2-1 and my confidence was back. With a quick leg kick and smooth release I evened the count at 2-2. I tried to put too much on the next pitch and the rising fastball sailed just high, making the count full. I didn't want to walk the batter so I eased up the velocity a bit on the 3-2 pitch. My changeup had the Blue Bombers number three-hitter swinging too soon and she pulled a laser down the left-field line. Thankfully, our third baseman, Laura Simpson was on her toes and snagged the sizzling shot for the third out. I sighed deeply, a sense of relief rushing over me like a warm shower.

We hustled into the dugout and I smiled from ear to ear, knowing that I'd passed my first test. I'd made it through one inning without getting bombed. Unfortunately, there was little time to celebrate. I had to grab a helmet and get ready to bat. I hit third in the lineup, which meant that I needed to quickly find my batting gloves (the ones given to me by Jose Valentine), and get ready to hit. Even though they were too big, I was sure that wearing them would give me a slugger's mentality.

Our first two batters made outs so I stepped up to the plate with the bases empty. I was content to watch a few pitches, hoping to get the rhythm of the opposing pitcher. The first two pitches came in pretty quick but both missed the strike zone. I knew the next one was going to be a strike. Sure enough, I was right. The 2-0 pitch came right down the middle and I pulled the trigger immediately after the ball was released. I took all of my frustration out on that swing. I had sat out of the game for over a year. Being back meant everything to me. My bat made solid contact, sending their left fielder deep down the line in pursuit. The ball continued to sail as if being propelled by an engine. The left fielder could only watch as the ball landed just inside the foul line and continued to roll through the endless outfield.

Meanwhile, I was heading toward second and had my mind set on third. As I raced around second base, I was sure I would be safe at third. And so was Coach Larry. He was so sure, that he was still waving as I made my way toward the bag. His arms signaled for me to keep my head down and keep running. He was sending me home to beat the throw! I pounced my foot on the third base bag and shoved off toward home just as their shortstop was receiving the cutoff throw from their left fielder.

I turned my head, and from the corner of my eye, I watched as she spun around and tossed one toward the plate. Right away, I noticed their catcher stepping away from me and toward the first-base line. The throw home was off line and I indented my cleat in the center of the plate, running into the arms of our excited cleanup hitter, Anne Fishburn. Although Anne struck out swinging to end the first, my home run had the scoreboard reading: Orange Crush 1, Blue Bombers 0.

We maintained our lead through the first five innings of the game, adding on three more runs. But the story of the day was happening on the pitcher's mound. Somehow, I had sailed through the first five innings without allowing one single hit, although I did walk two batters. Not giving up a hit seemed incredible, but my main focus was simply to finish the game and get the win. Not having played a full seven-inning game in over a year, let alone not having *ever* pitched a whole game, I hoped my stamina would carry me through to the finish line.

I started to get tired in the top of the sixth, walking the leadoff batter after throwing some pretty awful pitches. She advanced to second on a ground out and then to third on a sacrifice bunt. But I managed to strand her there when I reached back for an extra hot fastball, jamming the number nine hitter, who popped one up to shallow left field to end the inning.

I clenched my fist in excitement as I entered the dugout for the final sit down before the showdown. All I needed were three straight outs to collect a no-hitter. *Stay calm*, I thought, *stop thinking so much*. I sat next to Elizabeth for what seemed like an eternity, sipping from a cup of cool water and trying to clear my head of any negative thoughts. *Just keep pitching,* I told myself. Ten agonizing minutes later, we made our third out and I hustled to the mound with a 6-0 lead in the top of the seventh.

With a no-hitter on the line, I knew I really had to think about each pitch I threw. The truth was, I didn't know that much about pitching. Most of what I had done so far had been based on instinct. What I did know was that getting ahead of the hitters with early strikes had been the key to my success all day, so I made sure to groove the first pitch of the inning right down the middle of the plate. On the next pitch, I went for the inside corner and again the hitter stood frozen, strike two.

Although I never had any formal pitching training, I had watched enough Scorpions games to know that this was a situation where I could afford to waste a pitch. Even if I threw a ball, I would still be ahead of the hitter. Knowing this, I considered tossing one out of the strike zone and hoping she would swing at it. I also considered the fact that my arm felt limp and exhausted, so I decided that instead of wasting energy on a pitch out of the strike zone, I would try for the outside corner instead. My pitch sailed a little high and the hitter clubbed a soft line drive that looped right into the glove of our first baseman, Clara Manning, for an easy first out. "Good pitch, Selena." Elizabeth shouted from behind the plate.

I wiped a pool of sweat from my forehead. "One out!" I shouted to my teammates, holding up my pointer finger in the air. "Now I just need two more," I whispered. Wanting to maintain my focus, I kept my vision zeroed in on home plate. This was difficult, because it meant avoiding the chatter I could hear coming from our opponent's dugout and the buzz of the excited crowd in the stands.

Their number two batter was content to watch my first two pitches, resulting in a 1-1 count. The third pitch rolled off my fingertips oddly, sending the ball hopping toward the backstop. *What was that?* I wondered, taking a deep breath. On the fourth pitch, I thought I had caught the outside corner but the umpire disagreed, dropping the count to 3-1. I definitely didn't want to give in to this hitter with a "meat" pitch, so I went low and outside and hoped that I'd hit my spot.

The pitch was perfect and the batter dribbled one over to Clara Manning at second. She rushed in on the ball and fielded it cleanly, but as she went to make the easy throw over to first, she lost her footing and the ball sailed wide into our dugout. The runner advanced to second on the error, adding weight to my heavy burden. Clara dropped her head in disappointment. I turned and looked her directly in the eyes. "Hey, don't worry about it, Clara." I said these words aloud, but inside, my frustration was boiling over.

Although my no-hitter was still intact after Clara's error, I wasn't sure if I had enough power left in my right arm to get the final two outs. Then I remembered the mental exercises that I'd learned from reading Lefty Anderson's autobiography for the Readathon Challenge. I pulled my neon orange visor down over my closed eyes and visualized my windmill arm motion releasing a perfect strike. I flashed this picture in my mind over and over until I had forgotten about Clara, her error, the runner, and the crowd.

Moving toward the rubber I looked up at their number three batter, a power-hitting lefty who was crowding the plate. As the first pitch flew toward the plate she surprised me and squared around to bunt. The ball bounced off of her bat right in front of home plate and died. I knew there was no way I could reach it in time. *Oh no, I thought, you're gonna lose your no-hitter on a bunt!* Just as this thought went through my head, athletic and agile Elizabeth sprung out from behind home plate like a hungry cat. She circled the ball and tossed a bullet over to Clara at first. The runner was out by a thumbnail.

"Great play, Liz! Two outs!" Clara shouted, holding up two fingers.

Elizabeth's amazing play energized me and I scampered back to the rubber with a skip to my step. I pointed at Elizabeth excitedly, unable to speak after her heroics. I placed my glove to my heart and felt it pounding through my jersey top. My long hair was blowing in front of my face as I breathed another deep breath. I was one out away—one out away from a lifetime achievement. I toed the rubber and confidently stared into Elizabeth's glove.

My first offering zipped in and caught the inside corner of the plate, strike one. I barely took any time before unleashing my second pitch, which popped as it hit Elizabeth's glove for strike two. Now I was starting to feel the gravity of the moment. The crowd stood on their feet and I knew I had to step back. So I did, rubbing my foot over the mound again and again to calm my nerves.

As I ascended upon my throne again, the runner at third base started lunging up and down the line trying to break my concentration. I felt myself falling into the eye of a tornado as the crowd and the chatter on the field swirled all around me. I needed to find my focus one last time, and I knew exactly where to look. I slid my right hand, the hand that had developed calluses from months of pitching practice, into my back pocket. It was there that I felt the comfort of Mom's prayer card. I smiled thinking about her and immediately the butterflies disappeared, the tornado was replaced by the quiet peace of the Arizona sun and Mom's presence on the mound with me.

I peered up at Elizabeth, who pounded her glove. "Right here, Selena! One more strike!"

I followed her orders, delivering a perfect pitch for a storybook-ending strike three. Unfortunately, this wasn't a storybook. The Blue Bombers batter swung and connected. I watched as the ball floated off her bat and sailed toward shallow left field. *Oh no*, I thought.

I turned and watched helplessly as the sphere began to lose its steam just out of the reach of Anne Fishburn at short. I held my mitt near my face as I watched the ball begin its descent. I dreaded the predictable outcome. This one was definitely going to drop in.

Then, from out of nowhere, our left fielder, Shannon Edison, came running at the ball with a full head of steam. She wasn't going to give up on this one. *Come on Shannon,* I thought. "Get there Shannon!" I screamed, just as the ball reached head level. Shannon dropped into a feet-first slide. I started running toward the plate to back up our catcher in case of a throw home. I backpedaled from the mound, never taking my eyes off of Shannon as she rolled over twice and then jumped to her feet, holding in her hand the red-laced softball!

Three outs! Game over! My no-hitter was complete!

I sprinted out to Shannon in left and the dog pile quickly formed around us. The rest of my teammates joined the celebration. We rolled around like lunatics, blades of grass sticking in our hair and teeth.

The buzz around the Bobby Sox community revolved around my no-hitter for a week or so. The word even reached the neighboring town of La Mira, an area where softball superstars seemed to grow like cactus. At our third Orange Crush game of the season, about a week after my no-hitter, Victoria Joyce approached me. Victoria was a former college softball pitcher who grew up in La Mira, and was kind of a legend in Arizona's softball community. She was just twenty-three years old, but already was a respected coach. I guessed that she had heard about my accomplishment from one of her players.

Mom used to say that things never worked out the way you planned, but that if you had patience, they would work out all the same. I never planned for Mom to leave. I never planned on being a pitcher, and I certainly never planned on throwing a no-hitter. But in a strange twist of fate, a combination of all of these events brought a very special person into my life.

Victoria Joyce offered her hand to me in introduction. "Wow, congratulations on that no-hitter. I heard all about it." I smiled, still unsure of why Victoria was approaching me. "You know, I teach lessons to some of the best pitchers around here. I was wondering if you would be interested in coming out and practicing with us."

"Me?" I asked uncertain. "One of the best pitchers around here?" I cracked a half smile. "Really?"

"Sure. I mean, you definitely got everyone's attention last week. I heard you were untouchable." Something drew me toward Victoria immediately. She was in amazing physical shape for starters, not an ounce of fat showed on her 5-foot-10-inch frame. Yet her muscles did not match her soft and sweet personality. Despite the fact that she towered over me, her delicate combination of strength and sweetness represented the balance that I was constantly searching for in myself. She spoke with a pleasant tone, was always smiling and displayed lady-like features—from her soft pink T-shirt to her rose-painted fingernails. She even had a fancy bow that held up her sandy blond hair. After talking with her for about twenty seconds I knew that Victoria and Mom would have gotten along well. Of course, this made me like her even more. "What do you think, Selena?" Victoria continued.

"Well, I'll have to talk to my dad first." I knew that her lessons were going to cost money, and I knew that was going to cause a problem. "He's right over there." I pointed to the gate down by the right-field fence. I waved Dad over and he joined us near the dugout.

The two of them shook hands and I twisted my long black hair around my finger, wondering if Victoria would be able to convince Dad that he needed to spend his hard earned money on pitching lessons for his daughter. I let the two of them talk for awhile, standing about ten feet away from them—just close enough so that

I could catch the gist of the conversation. Victoria jumped right in, giving Dad all the information and financial requirements. Dad seemed interested and kept saying, "That would be great." He explained that he loved that I was involved with softball again and that the pitching lessons sounded awesome. Dad was also very honest, letting Victoria know that money was a major obstacle for us. After all, Victoria charged $20 an hour, which was as much as Dad made in an hour! When I heard that number, I was sure Dad would tell Victoria no thank you, and I would probably never see her again. But that's not what happened.

For some reason, Dad became pretty comfortable with Victoria too, and the two of them sat down in the dugout and talked for about an hour. I tossed the ball around with Anne Fishburn just a few feet away as Dad shared the story of Mom's death and explained to Victoria how hard it had been on our family. Victoria listened compassionately. After speaking to Dad a little bit longer, Victoria came up with an idea—she had figured out a way that she could waive the fee.

She called me over excitedly and we discussed a way for me to work off her coaching fee. Victoria worked every day as a student teacher, then she coached games for the junior varsity team and *then* she went to school at nights to get her teaching credentials. Her problem was that her dog, Sammy, was home alone all day. She needed someone to walk him. And as it turned out, although Victoria taught in La Mira, she lived in Tierra de Sueño, about three blocks from my house. She had planned on hiring someone to walk her dog, but like Mom always said, "plans hardly ever turn out the way you plan them."

Within ten seconds, I told Victoria how much I loved dogs

71

and how happy I would be to walk Sammy every day after school. So in a stroke of luck—we struck a deal.

Two days later, I arrived at my first session. For the next hour Victoria showed me things I'd never even heard of or thought about. She started with the basics, teaching me a special stretch to loosen up my pitching arm. By holding my arm at a strange angle for a few seconds, I was able to stretch muscles I never even knew I had. Then she showed me the proper way to position my toes on the pitching rubber, so that on set-up, they pointed towards my target. This allowed for greater push off and accuracy. She really stressed the importance of the follow through and the drag foot, which helped to direct the ball. Most of the stuff she talked about, I had been doing all wrong. I'm not even sure if I knew my feet had anything to do with pitching before I started working with Victoria. After all, I had learned how to pitch by pitching. Although I was pretty good, I would never be able to reach my full potential without learning the fundamentals. In those first sixty minutes, Victoria taught me more about pitching than I had learned in my thirteen years of life. Amazingly, it was fun.

Victoria's instructions were crystal. The repetition of skills never became tedious either because she flavored them with her own personal stories. She told me about the day she was late for high school practice and rushed on the field, not taking time to stretch. After her first pitch she felt a twinge of pain—a pulled muscle in her arm ended up sidelining her for two months. She shared all kinds of stories, each one relating to the game and to life in a different way. After just a few sessions together, Victoria's mental approach to softball was rubbing off on me. I was starting to see the game completely differently. Under her careful watch I had adopted the mindset of a pitcher. And under my watch, Sammy the dog was no longer peeing in Victoria's living room.

CHAPTER SEVEN

A BUMPY RIDE

For the next six months, that's how it went for me. Victoria continued to offer me free pitching instruction and I continued to improve. I became so comfortable with Victoria that I openly shared my thoughts regarding Mom's death, thoughts I didn't share with anyone but her. Every other Saturday, while my brothers tiptoed around potholes on the Field and Dad struggled to make ends meet by working overtime, I was learning how to throw a curveball and a drop pitch. I was also making a friend for life. The wounds that remained from Mom's death were beginning to heal more and more every day. This wasn't the way I'd planned it, but everything was working out—just like Mom said it would.

One day, during one of my pitching lessons, the rain started pouring down on Victoria and I. Now, where you live, this may be a common occurrence, but in the Arizona desert, when it rains, you're never prepared. So the rain poured down in buckets and we sat stranded in the dugout, watching the dusty infield dirt turn to dark brown mud. As the rain splashed on top of the dugout, and drops fell through the cracks and onto our heads, Victoria shared a story with me. It was then that I realized the true reason Victoria had been helping me for free over the past six months. Sure, the daily walks I took Sammy on were a big help to Victoria, but there was another reason she had been so touched by my story. As it turned out, we had more in common than I thought.

Victoria explained, with tears trickling down her cheeks, that she, too, had lost a parent at an early age. For her, it was her father, Phil, who had passed away. Just like me, she'd had a difficult time getting back into life after that. That was why she decided to help me in the first place, because she knew what I was going through. I couldn't believe she had waited six months to tell me that story, but when she did I felt closer to her than ever. As she finished talking and wiped the tears from her eyes, the rain stopped. We both stood up and made our way out onto the muddy field in time to see a rainbow form in the clouds above us. I pitched to Victoria in the mud with the rainbow as a backdrop, knowing that Mom and Phil were smiling somewhere, watching their girls play ball together.

Although days like that meant the most to me, the really fun part of my training was on game days when I was able to bring all my new skills to the pitcher's mound for the Orange Crush. By season's end, I had pitched in eight games and we had lost only once. More importantly, I was experiencing major improvements every time I stepped onto the mound. Sure, there were some setbacks, but overall I was happy with my progression.

Under Victoria's watchful eye I became one of the top fourteen-and-under pitchers in Bobby Sox and began playing on a traveling team in the off-season as well. Victoria said that if I worked hard enough at it, softball could be my ticket to a free college education. With high school approaching in just two short months, my focus shifted to attaining that very goal. After all, anything I could do to help Dad financially was just fine by me. Especially if all I had to do was continue to play softball, pitch and improve my game.

In high school softball, the games meant a whole lot more than they did in Bobby Sox. There were section titles to be captured, playoff games to be played, and school pride to be demonstrated. It wasn't uncommon for college scouts to show up to these games, searching for the best of the best, and offering these special players scholarships to attend their schools. The question was whether I would be one of them. Up until this point, softball had always come easy to me. Still, I wondered if I was ready to be the best at Monte Vista High School.

A few months later, while walking the halls of Monte Vista on my first day as a high school freshman, I couldn't believe how fast time had traveled. It seemed like yesterday that I had been a ten-year-old girl, playing youth baseball with the boys and screaming at my brothers on the Field. I was now fourteen years old, just four years away from college.

To be totally honest, high school wasn't nearly as intimidating as I had expected it to be. Unlike my transition to middle school, I made some new friends easily and adjusted quickly to high school. The schoolwork, though, was definitely harder at Monte Vista. Now that I was a freshman I was expected to take more tests and complete longer homework assignments. I kept my grades a top priority in my life, neck-and-neck with softball. And I was able to maintain a high B average. I knew that if I kept my grades up I would have more options when it came time to choose a college.

When spring came around I tried out for the varsity softball squad and actually made it. Anne Fishburn and I were the only two freshmen who earned spots on the team. The coach, Mrs. Moody, tagged me as the number two pitcher behind senior wind-miller Michelle Sierra. I didn't mind the secondary role, especially since Michelle had three years of varsity experience under her belt. Mrs. Moody, on the other hand, had no softball experience under her belt. A physical education teacher, Mrs. Moody was generally knowledgeable in sports. Yet, when it came to the ins and outs of softball—she didn't have a clue. She took the coaching position as a favor to our principal when the long-time varsity coach quit a week before tryouts.

The only information Mrs. Moody got about softball came from a thick manual, which she rolled up and kept with her at all times. It became a joke to us players, and we even gave the book our own title, "Softball for Dummies."

Unfortunately, Mrs. Moody's philosophy was always "by the book," never wavering from the text's suggestions. If a runner reached base with no outs, the next hitter always had to bunt her over. Why? Because the book said so. If you were pitching to the cleanup batter with a runner on, and fell behind 3-0, you had to intentionally walk her. Why? Because the book said so. If the batter was right handed and a runner on first tried to steal second, the second baseman was the only one allowed to cover the base. Why? Because the book said so. This coaching style sucked the fun and excitement right out of the game for all of us. Although her book offered good advice, we all knew that softball was not an exact science. Adjustments needed to be made on-the-fly, risks needed to be taken, and an occasional surprise had to be thrown at an opponent in order to be successful.

At six-foot-two-inches tall and close to two hundred pounds, Mrs. Moody was a physical force to be reckoned with. Her loud voice and permanent mean expression made her extra intimidating. She also ran a very tight ship. If you were late for practice, even by one minute, you had to run ten wind sprints in the outfield. If you missed a practice and weren't excused, you sat out a game. And if you missed a sign during a game you had to put away the entire load of practice equipment into a shed, which was fifty yards from the field. This boot camp approach didn't sit well with me. I preferred positive encouragement and pats on the back. After all, I was my own toughest critic, beating myself up when I made a mistake. Mrs. Moody only added to my frustration. Like a highlighter pen, she accented my errors, making them more noticeable.

Making friends with new teammates, like my catcher Monica Larson, helped soften the disappointment of a season under the thumb of Coach Moody. Our games were about as fun as chewing on tinfoil and our practices were ten times worse than that. In club softball, under Coach Larry and Coach Wilson, I had a great time and we won too. Directed by Mrs. Moody, we failed in both of those departments.

Personally, my freshman season could have been a lot worse. I pitched fairly well despite our team's ridiculous record. I gave up only about three earned runs a game, but teams averaged close to six against me due to poor fielding.

My frustration peaked with only five games left in the regular season. Our team, the Monarchs, had won a horrible four of twenty games as we headed into a contest against our crosstown rival, the Del Rey Cougars. I started the game and pitched solid through the first three innings of a scoreless tie. In the top of the fourth, however, the Cougars managed to collect two runs off me. The leadoff batter laid down a perfect drag bunt up the first-base line, beating the throw by an inch.

The next hitter, Kim McMann, was the Cougars' feared cleanup batter. As I looked at my catcher, Monica Larson, she signaled for the rise ball. I shook my head at her, trying to get a new sign. Having played against Kim in club softball, I knew she loved the high stuff. I also knew, having played almost a full season under Coach Moody, that when Monica peered over to the dugout to get another sign, Moody would never budge. Sure enough, Mrs. Moody called for a rise ball, once again. So I dug the ball deep into my glove and gripped my fingers along the seams for a rise ball—again.

I sighed deeply and threw the pitch, knowing it wouldn't be successful. I executed it to perfection. The ball rose out of my right hand just as it was supposed to. And then it rose right off of Kim's bat into the right centerfield gap, scoring the speedy runner all the way from first to make the score: Cougars 1, Monarchs 0. I shook my head in frustration as the ball was thrown back to me from the outfield. I knew these batters better than our coach, yet she demanded to be in control.

With Kim on second base after a booming double, I struck out the next batter on pure fire, throwing 'frustration fastballs' past their fifth hitter. Next, the Cougars sent up Mercy Reyes, who normally batted from the right side. But for this at bat she decided to switch over to the left. I knew her plan immediately. Mercy was going to start as far back in the batter's box as was possible without bumping into the umpire, run toward the pitch and slap it down into the ground as hard as she could. This was called a slap bunt and was much more effective when applied by a left-handed batter. Standing on the right side of the plate would give Mercy a quick exit out of the box and a head start down the first-base line.

Aware of the high probability of the slap bunt, my mind instantly registered the pitch selection needed. If I kept the ball up so Mercy couldn't pound it down into the ground, and kept the ball outside so she couldn't exit the box early, I would completely nullify her advantage. That equated to a rise ball on the outside of the plate. I eyed Monica's glove for the sign: drop ball. "Great call Mrs. Moody," I whispered under my breath sarcastically. I bent down to my cleats, faking like I needed to retie my laces. I couldn't believe Mrs. Moody's mindset! She had absolutely no understanding of pitch selection. *Why is she calling the shots, anyway?* I thought.

I flung my long hair away from my face and stepped back on the mound, hoping Monica would flash a new sign. But I had no such luck. I shook my head at Monica, indicating my displeasure. Then I heard a booming voice call out to me angrily from the dugout, "Quit shaking me off, Selena!" Mrs. Moody shouted loud enough for everyone to hear—my teammates, the opposing team and even the fans. Now that everyone was aware of the power struggle between Coach Moody and myself, my face flashed red in embarrassment.

Making sure not to make eye contact with my angry coach, I slid my fingers over the ball and dug my left toe into the rubber. I'd throw the drop ball, but I was keeping it outside. Frustrated, I executed the pitch poorly and the ball spun out of my fingers and landed in the dirt on the outside half of the plate. It slipped under Monica's glove, allowing Kim to advance from second to third.

"Ugghh!" I muttered under my breath. I was so frustrated by Mrs. Moody that I had gotten completely out of my rhythm. On the next pitch, she called for a drop ball again. Mercy had an easy time making contact with this one. She bounced the low pitch into the dirt, and raced to first with a single. Kim scored from third easily to make the score Cougars 2, Monarchs 0.

When the ball returned to my glove I waved Monica toward me at the mound. She arrived, and I looked at her brown eyes through the bars of her face mask, speaking in a sharp whisper. "I don't care what Mrs. Moody calls. We're throwing rise balls to the next batter because she's gonna try and drag bunt, too. And the next batter after that we're throwing fastballs because she can't catch up to them. You got it?" My competitive juices were flowing now and my frustration was apparent in my body language. I was embarrassing myself out here and it was all Mrs. Moody's fault. If she couldn't make the right calls, I would. Monica stared back at me and nodded her helmet-heavy head in agreement.

My game plan worked to perfection as the next batter popped up my rise ball for the second out and the eighth hitter struck out watching my fastball pop into Monica's glove. Calling my own pitches and getting two easy outs didn't ease my frustrations—my success only fueled them more.

When I got to the dugout, I walked right past Mrs. Moody and threw my mitt under the bench in disgust, grabbing a helmet and walking over to the on-deck circle to warm up. I was the lead-off batter in the inning and had to hustle.

Before I reached the plate, Mrs. Moody hollered toward the end of the bench, "Traci, get a bat! You're pinch-hitting for Selena." Then she looked directly at me, "Selena, have a seat."

I froze in my tracks. "But Coach, I—"

She cut me off before I could explain to her why I had called my own pitches last inning. "There's only one coach on this team, Selena, and it's not you." Her voice was cold and her eyes were dark as she stared straight at me. "Now have a seat."

By disobeying Mrs. Moody on the pitcher's mound, I had really made her mad. She didn't care that I had the second-best batting average on the team. She didn't care that the score was still close in this game. She wouldn't even let me convince her that I *needed* to bat in order to help our team to win. As I found my way to the far end of the dugout, Traci had already dug her cleats into the batter's box. I set my bat against the fence, took off my Jose Valentine batting gloves and sat down on the hardwood bench.

A few of my teammates slid next to me and asked the same questions that spun around in my head: *Who would pitch the next inning? Does she want to lose?* The truth was, she didn't care about the outcome of the game. What she cared about was that I got her message—"There's only one coach on this team, and it's not you." Sitting on the bench with tears in my eyes, that message was ringing through loud and clear.

The next inning Coach Moody brought in our right fielder, Lisa Wilkins, to pitch, even though she'd only thrown in two games all season. Lisa had a tough time finding the strike zone, allowing six runs that inning and four more the next. We lost that game by a final score of 15-1.

When I came home after the game, I grabbed Mom's pillow and ran into her room. I laid on the bed all alone, crying. Although nearly four years had passed since her death, Mom's sweet fragrance still remained deep in the heart of the pillow. No matter how long she had been, her absence never got any easier. Especially when I was upset.

Luckily, there was another presence in my life to help me get through tough times. In the middle of my sobs the knock on the front door was a welcome sound. Victoria, who had stopped by to hear how the game went, was standing at the front door. Unfortunately, she had not been able to come to the game because of her night class. My red eyes clued her into the fact that the ship hadn't sailed smoothly. We sat together in the kitchen and shared a bowl of cookie dough ice cream. In her usual way, Victoria listened intently to my complaints about Mrs. Moody and about my horrible first season of high school softball. I told her that I was thinking about quitting the team and that I couldn't handle playing for Mrs. Moody any longer.

In between spoonfuls, Victoria offered her advice. "I totally understand your frustration." She put her arm on my shoulder in sympathy. "Mrs. Moody definitely has a *different* coaching style and she doesn't make all the right choices. Still, she *is* your coach. And when you joined the team, you made the decision to play under her guidance. Sounds like you got into a power struggle today. Selena, Mrs. Moody, with all her faults, *is* the boss. You won't win that battle." She lifted both her palms up in a matter-of-fact manner. Mom used to do the same thing, and for a moment I felt her in the room with us. A lump of ice cream slid down my throat. I was choked up and tried to squeeze back the tears, but a few rolled down my cheek anyway. Victoria took the napkin off the table and dried the drops. "I went through some tough times with coaches, too. I hated my college coach. He'd yell at me and criticize me and make stupid coaching mistakes. Believe me, I thought about quitting. But sticking with softball turned out to be a great decision for me. You're not a quitter either, Selena." Victoria smiled. "Besides, you know you can't *really* quit, anyway. You love it way too much."

As I sat there eating spoonful after spoonful of ice cream, I realized that Victoria was absolutely right. Sure, high school softball had been a bumpy ride so far, but there was no way I could ever quit playing the sport I loved so much. I would just have to deal with Mrs. Moody. Eventually, I'd get a coach that I actually liked. The question was—when?

CHAPTER EIGHT

TWO SURPRISES

With about a week left in my freshman softball season, I got ready to celebrate my fifteenth birthday. Dad told me that we were going to have a small party at a local reception hall, and that he was going to invite about ten people to join us. This sounded like fun to me and seemed like a great way to get my mind off of Mrs. Moody for a while. There were just three games left in our regular season at this point, but only one in which I was slated to pitch. I know it sounds bad, but I was actually relieved that the softball season was ending.

Victoria volunteered to drive me down to the hall because Dad said he wouldn't be able to meet us until after work. As we pulled into the parking lot, I wondered if Dad had invited any girls from my team. "That would be cool," I told Victoria, "because us girls rarely get the chance to talk about anything but softball. This would be a great chance for us to sit down and talk without a bunch of people around and all the pressure of the game on our shoulders—just a bunch of girls eating pizza and hanging out." Victoria smiled at my comments.

We casually walked toward the front door and I opened it without a second thought.

"Surprise!"

Bright lights flashed as I stepped through the door. After my eyes had adjusted to the flashing lights, I smiled brightly and turned a deep cherry red. The room seemed to spin in circles as everyone that I had ever known in my entire life stood in front of me, packed into this beautifully decorated hall, celebrating my birthday. I had never been so surprised or excited. The loud cheers, whistling and clapping were all directed at me! Standing in shock at the hall's entrance, I looked toward a stage situated on the other side of the room. There, hanging in between loads of gold and white balloons, was a sign with the words: "Happy Birthday Selena!"

One glance at my golf-ball sized eyes and shocked stare confirmed that I was surprised. Dad was the first person to meet me at the door as I walked through it. Dressed in a navy blue suit and tie, he wrapped his big arms around me and pressed his lips against my cheek. When he drew away, his eyes welled up with tears as he gently held my face in his hands. "This is your day, baby girl!"

It was my fifteenth birthday, which meant that it was time for my quinceañera. The quinceañera is a celebration of a girl's entrance into womanhood—Hispanic girls all over the world celebrate this occasion. Dad and I had talked about this day a month earlier and he said that we would skip the formalities of the event and just have some pizza with my friends. Boy, did he fool me. This was not only a real quinceañera party, but Dad had pulled out all the stops—from elaborate decorations, to the band that was setting up in the corner. I had no idea how much planning Dad had done to make this day great for me.

I squeezed my arms around his waist as a flood of emotions streamed through my body. Some aroused tears of sadness, some tears of joy and some tears of relief. Following Mom's death, Dad had made a change in his priorities, appreciating his parenting role more deeply. He had worked with his boss and shifted his work hours as much as possible, attending as many of our sporting events and school activities as were possible. At home, he spent quality time talking with my brothers and me about our lives. We had even convinced him to play in a few games at the Field.

As Dad and I released our embrace, he handed me a beautiful pink gown. Pink is the traditional color a girl wears at her quinceañera. Victoria looked over at me and smiled. I assumed she had helped Dad pick out the dress. My eyes lit up as I ran my fingers down the delicately laced fabric. "Wow! It's beautiful!" I kissed Dad on the cheek and shot a knowing smile toward Victoria.

Victoria led me to the girl's restroom, where I changed out of my jeans, T-shirt and tennis shoes, and into the gown and ballerina slippers. Then, Victoria worked to apply the finishing touches, adding a few curls to my hair and brightening my face with blush, mascara and rose lipstick.

I exited the bathroom and entered the hall, bowing my head in embarrassment as the fifty-plus people hooted, howled and cheered at my appearance. All of the party guests headed down a small corridor to a room Dad had set up for the special ceremony, which is a part of a quinceañera. I never liked being the center of attention, but I got through the ceremony much like I got through my first appearance on the pitcher's mound. I knew everyone was looking at me and I managed to keep my chin up and not look too nervous. I should have been used to being the center of attention by now. After all, I had been playing a spotlight position on the softball field nearly every day for the past three years.

Following the service, I greeted all the guests as we reentered the reception hall. Their faces represented so many different phases of my life, especially those related to softball. There was Coach Frank Fisher from my first baseball team, Coach Larry from the Orange Crush softball squad, and tons of my former teammates, including our star shortstop Anne Fishburn and my catchers Elizabeth Lee and Monica Larson. Family flooded around me, too. Joe and Carlos and some of my cousins from Mexico were all in attendance.

A live band started the festivities off with a special dedicated song. The first dance of the quinceañera is traditionally shared by the birthday girl and her father. So Dad and I stepped out on the dance floor together. As he held me tight and slowly waltzed me around the room, all the guests encircled us, snapping pictures and swaying to the beat.

Traditionally, the second dance is set aside for the birthday girl and her boyfriend, but since I kept most of the boys at a distance, my brothers ran out on the dance floor. In typical teasing fashion, they fought over me until my older brother, Joe, won. After Joe dipped and spun me dizzy, Carlos traded spots with him and finished the song with the same melodramatic style. I smiled, laughed and screamed more than ever before during a two-minute song.

Following our dance, the band announced the need to perform another ritual. I sat down in a chair in the middle of a circle of people, stretching my feet out from under my floor-length dress. Dad explained that he would be removing my ballerina slippers and replacing them with high heels, symbolizing the change from childhood to womanhood. I dropped my head back, stared at the ceiling and belted out an embarrassed laugh. High heels were not in my wardrobe!

Before Dad could slip on the pink, satin heels, Victoria entered the circle and interrupted the custom. "Excuse me Mr. Garcia, can I make a slight change?" Dad had obviously shared in this prank, as he eagerly stepped out of the way. Victoria knelt down, set her shoebox on the ground, and lifted off the top. With a grin she revealed to the crowd a pair of brand-new, shiny, black leather cleats. The room erupted in laughter as Victoria slipped them onto my feet.

Playing along with the joke, I pranced around like a model strutting down the runway. As I hammed it up with the crowd, I felt a sense of freedom inside of me. I really *was* turning into a woman. Quietly, I had always feared that after Mom passed away I would never learn how to be elegant, beautiful or ladylike. After all, what did Dad or Joe or Carlos know about that stuff?

The evening continued on with great conversations, dancing, delicious food and traditional desserts. The band serenaded me with a Spanish rendition of Happy Birthday—*Feliz Compleaño*—before I blew out all fifteen candles. The final event of the night served as more than icing on the cake. While I stood chatting with Anne and Elizabeth, Dad walked over and politely interrupted. Most of the guests migrated over to us, sensing a special moment. Dad reached inside his suit jacket and pulled out a small, wrapped box. He handed it to me and smiled. The music stopped for a moment. "This is for you, Selena."

Stunned, I cradled the box in my hand like an egg. I looked back at my dad, shyly tilting my head. "Dad, what are you doing? This party was supposed to be my gift."

"Just open it, Selena." Dad smiled.

I pulled off the white satin ribbon and slowly peeled back the shiny wrapping paper, revealing a black velvet box. I opened the box carefully, and there, shining as bright as a star in the dark of night, was Mom's wedding ring. In the center of the simple setting sparkled a small, round diamond, surrounded by gold. It was beautiful.

I elevated my eyes to Dad, unable to speak my emotions. I could only wrap my arms around him again as I began to cry. Dad, too, was weeping as he whispered into my ear, "Your mother was an amazing person," he paused to regain his composure, "and you're more like her every day." Again he paused, barely able to speak without crying, "She would want you to wear this."

Although I still missed Mom and wished she could have been there to witness my celebration, the love that surrounded me that night filled me with happiness. I knew that my journey into womanhood wouldn't be easy, but I was determined to use that joyful birthday memory to continually inspire me to live up to Mom's legacy.

Two weeks after my party, I completed my freshman softball season, earning my first varsity letter as a member of the Monte Vista High team. There were times throughout that season when I had vowed to never play the sport again. But I had made it through that first year with the drill sergeant, Mrs. Moody, and I was still standing, ready for another season under her "expert" guidance. I wasn't going to let her stop me from attaining my dream.

Luckily, miracles do happen. The summer before my sophomore year, I found out that I would never have to deal with Mrs. Moody again. Talk about a great surprise! Victoria had just received a teaching position at Monte Vista High. And, what was even better was that Mrs. Moody decided she didn't want to coach the softball team again next year. Principal Hill quickly offered the varsity softball coaching job to his new freshman English teacher, Victoria Joyce!

With a familiar flowerbed to flourish in, I was ready to blossom. The first day of school couldn't come soon enough. Seeing Victoria with her teacher's ID badge hanging from her neck was a sweet sight, but seeing her hold a clipboard on the softball field while wearing a maroon Monarchs sweatshirt fired me up even more.

Even though it was only fall and my sophomore season was nearly six months away, I spent every day after school down on the diamond. Our catcher Monica Larson, myself, and our first baseman Lisa Irwin, helped Victoria revamp the field, raking the new dirt in the infield and planting seeds in the outfield where patches of grass had turned brown. The field definitely needed a facelift and we felt like makeup artists as we touched up the dugout benches, pulled weeds along the backstop and repaired broken fences in the outfield.

The biggest transformation came in the batting cage, which we had affectionately tagged "The Dungeon." Pieces of net hung down all over the small, chain link enclosed area. Often times in our back swings we would get our bats stuck in a piece of netting.

Dozens of balls would get caught in the loose webbing. This was why we had to wear helmets, because at any time one of the stray balls could drop right down on someone's head. We assisted Victoria in tying back the loose nets, smoothing out the footing, and oiling up the rickety pitching machine.

Our reward for helping Victoria was huge. At any time, outside of class time of course, we could get the key to the batting cage and hit for as long as we wanted. Our team was able to swing away in the new cage. We even came up with our own scoring system, labeling each bat-to-ball connection as a hit or an out. The workouts were pure fun. I hit more balls that off-season than I had in all my years of playing softball combined, and it showed once the regular season began.

The first game of my sophomore season was a dominating victory for the Monarchs. I pitched a shutout, striking out six and walking just one. Plus, I finished 3-for-4 with a double and two RBI's. I couldn't have asked for a better start.

That entire sophomore season was like a dream I didn't want to wake up from. With Victoria running the show, our team posted the best record in school history, 15-6, and finished second in our league. Although we lost early in the playoffs, our accomplishments far outnumbered our mistakes.

People at school began recognizing the softball team as we became one of the top programs. And people began recognizing me. Fellow coaches and players started asking about my future plans with the sport. I hadn't given it too much thought, aside from knowing that I wanted a scholarship. The truth was, college seemed very far away to me. But when I came home from school one day at the end of my sophomore year, a look through the mailbox made me realize that college was right around the corner.

Hidden in the middle of grocery ads and junk mail, was a letter addressed to me from the University of Horizon. I opened up the stiff, parchment letter and read the words "...interested in you as a college softball student-athlete." For the first time in my sixteen years of life I realized that my athletic talent actually had a real chance of getting me somewhere—like college.

The letters continued to trickle in, following a successful season. When my junior year began, college coaches started to frequent our games, usually sitting in the stands right behind the dugout. They were easily within my view as I operated on the mound. I couldn't believe that coaches from around the country were showing up at the Monte Vista high softball field to watch *me* play!

Having been through the grueling recruiting process herself, Victoria knew exactly how to handle the stressful situation. She never told me before any of our games if scouts or coaches were coming, but she always informed me afterward. She bought our catcher Monica Larson a reflector strip to stick in the pocket of her glove, helping me blur out the fans in the background and focus only on her mitt. Although these tricks were great, the most effective tool I had against the pressure was planted in my back pocket. Victoria understood the power of Mom's prayer card, and helped me use that inspiration at the times I needed it most. When I seemed frazzled on the field or struggling in a slump, Victoria would pat her back pocket. This always reminded me that I was playing a *game* and that no matter where softball took me, Mom would be proud. This usually eased the tension I was feeling, and although it didn't always result in me throwing the perfect pitch or hitting a home run, it certainly put things into perspective.

Six years after her death, I still longed to touch my mother, often times crying at her absence. Yet, while I still refused to pull my hair up in a ponytail or tie it with bows and ribbons, I found myself becoming softer on the inside and more joyful on the outside. Dad was right—I was becoming more like Mom each day. I even started cooking some of her specialties in the kitchen for the boys. Seeing the looks on their faces, especially Dad's, when I pulled the tamales out of the oven the way Mom used to, made it all worthwhile. Like Mom, I began to appreciate the simple things—dinner dates with Dad, slumber parties with my teammates, long talks with my honorary big sister, Victoria, and even an occasional movie night with Joe and Carlos.

On the softball field, Victoria's competitive attitude drove me. Her coaching style brought out the best in me, which was clearly evident in the final game of that season, my best overall performance of the year.

Although we missed the playoffs by one game, we finished on a high note. I allowed just one unearned run in the season finale, fanning ten batters and walking none. We won the game 8-1 and I scored three of the runs and knocked in two others with a home run. I completed the season with a 12-3 record and batted .454, thanks primarily to all the extra work in the revamped batting cage. I earned another patch for my letterman's jacket as I was named a member of the first team All-County squad.

Following the final game, three college coaches stood along the first baseline fence, waiting to talk with me.

My teammates, especially seniors Monica Larson and Roselee Rivera, teased me as we cleaned up our gear. "Hey, looks like you've got a fan club, Selena." Roselee pushed me gently in the back.

Monica giggled. "Yeah, how much did you pay them to come today, huh?"

Victoria spoke to the trio of coaches before introducing me to each of them separately. All the coaches congratulated me on a great season and expressed interest in my future plans. They each offered me a recruiting visit to their campus next fall. Taking a recruiting visit doesn't necessarily guarantee a scholarship, but it is the final step before a school offers a player a scholarship.

I responded just as Victoria had prepared me to. I gave a solid, confident handshake, attentively listened and looked them directly in the eyes as I graciously said, "Thank you." Most importantly, Victoria told me that only six recruiting visits were allowed by the college athletics board, so I knew I could not commit to anything until all my options were laid out on the table.

To pretend I wasn't excited, though, would be like a bear saying he didn't like honey. The thought of playing *college* softball blew me away. No one in my family had ever attended a four-year college, let alone attended for free! Going to college on a softball scholarship seemed even more amazing, more fantastic.

The dream of getting a scholarship drove me daily. I couldn't go twenty-four hours without swinging a bat or throwing a ball. I spent the final month of my junior year swinging in the cage and pitching hundreds of balls per day. At home, much of my free time consisted of looking through a shoebox that I'd filled with recruiting letters. I lined up the notes alphabetically and devised a list of my top ten schools, which seemed to change with the wind. I was soon to find out that the winds of change can bite you.

CHAPTER NINE

CINDERELLA SUPERESTRELLA

On the last day of my junior year, I suited up for my final physical education class. LuAnn Gores, our starting catcher next season, was in that class, too. We had spent a good deal of that semester playing basketball, which was LuAnn's best sport. She was great at hoops. Although I knew she was superior on the hardwood, I still felt I was her equal when it came down to raw speed. So when she challenged me to a race across the floor at the end of class, I gladly obliged.

Most of the other students had left the gym and were headed for the locker room, but a handful of girls who knew us stuck around. Even our teacher, Mr. Silva, watched from the sideline. He was interested in the friendly competition between two of the school's top athletes. When Mr. Silva blew his whistle LuAnn and I both blasted off the baseline. We agreed to run one "suicide," which means running to the free-throw line and back, the half-court line and back, the far free-throw line and back, and finally, running the full court and back.

I reached the first free-throw line before LuAnn and raced back to the baseline, but right as I planted my right foot to pivot and turn back down the court my shoe stuck to the floor. My momentum carried me awkwardly over my foot and a snapping sound echoed through the gym as my ankle rolled sideways. Instantly, I fell to the floor and grabbed my right ankle with both hands, writhing in pain.

The cheers and jeers echoing throughout the gym fell silent. LuAnn's footsteps and my whimpering provided the only traces of noise. Mr. Silva quickly ran to my aid. "Are you alright, Selena?" He knelt down and tried to roll me over, but I planted my face into the floor trying to muffle my agony.

"It really, really hurts." I moaned as tears streamed down my cheeks.

LuAnn responded, "I'll run and get Victoria."

Mr. Silva convinced me to sit upright as he sent another student to fetch a bag of ice from the locker room. The pain in my ankle was as severe as any physical pain I could remember. This confirmed my gut feeling, which told me this injury was bad. Within two minutes, Victoria came running through the gym doors, breathing heavily. She immediately bent down beside me and put her hand on my back, gently rubbing it like a windshield wiper. "What happened, Selena?"

I paused, trying to clear my throat of all the tears. Dropping my head into my lap, I blubbered, "I think I just lost my scholarship."

My stupid race with LuAnn left me with a partially torn tendon in my right ankle and a giant, smelly, annoying and *not* softball-friendly cast. Lying helpless on the corduroy couch in our living room became a common occurrence for me during the summer before my senior year. Although three months had passed since the injury, my armpits still ached from the uncomfortable crutches and my body grew weary from lugging around the plaster boot day after day.

As news of my injury spread, many of the collegiate softball programs that were hot on my trail dropped interest in me altogether. The mailman placed fewer and fewer letters in our box, as the softball recruiting notes dwindled down to just one. Jason Lebot from the College of the Pines was the only coach who continued writing me on a consistent basis. He would send me handwritten notes about once a month. Coach Jason continually expressed concern for my wellbeing, but he never went as far as offering a recruiting visit to his school.

His interest represented my only hope at a scholarship. This hope, coupled with Victoria's constant support, made it impossible for me to give up. Every day during that summer Victoria picked me up at home and brought me to work with her at Monte Vista High. I knew that I was fighting against the odds, but I wouldn't quit until I was back on the pitcher's mound. So while Victoria taught summer school, I spent my days working out in the small gym—despite the hindrance of my annoying ankle cast. Sometimes I lifted weights for my upper body and other times I slowly rode the stationary bike, trying to maintain as much of my conditioning as possible. On some afternoons Victoria took me down on the field and I hit buckets of balls off a tee. Other days we simply played catch together. Doing anything softball related made me feel great.

Late at night, my ankle would hurt pretty badly. The cast wrapped around my leg seemed like the heaviest weight on earth, and being injured was really hard on me. I knew that if I could have just avoided that stupid race, I would probably have a college scholarship right now. Thoughts like these kept me awake some nights. They also propelled me to work twice as hard when I trained.

Keeping my pitching arm sharp proved to be the most difficult part of my grueling training. I could stand and throw overhand without much of a problem, but the windmill motion of pitching required too much lower body strength. It wasn't until the final two weeks of summer that I decided to step on the mound with my cast and try a few pitching reps. Forced to stand upright, the ball came off my hand wildly, and I found little control without my lower body's assistance. I threw about twenty pitches a day just to keep my arm loose and my shoulder rotation smooth, but without my legs, my workouts were limited. I have never doubted myself more than I did on those days. Tossing terrible pitch after terrible pitch, I'd wonder whether the problem was with me or with the cast wrapped tightly around my ankle.

Finally the day came to get that stupid, uncomfortable thing off my leg. As I sat on the doctor's table I felt like a prisoner about to be freed from jail. Dr. Brooks, my doctor since I was a little kid, used a special rotating saw to cut off the plaster molding. Underneath the cotton gauze wrap was my stiff right ankle and a tiny, shrunken calf muscle. The smell of my right leg and the long, black hair twisted around it nearly made me throw up. A shower and a shave became my first priority.

My next priority was rehab. Thank goodness Victoria believed in me so much. With my confidence dwindling after so many months of frustration and inactivity, it was hard for me to believe I would ever be the same pitcher I was prior to my injury. Her encouragement was the only thing that got me through the intense rehab portion on my road to recovery. I not only had to perform exercises and stretches four times a day, but I needed to regain my conditioning. Victoria, myself, and a few of my teammates ran sprints in the outfield every day during the off-season. This helped me get my wind back pretty quickly. That, and some repetitions in the batting cage had me thinking positively by midwinter.

Although it proved to be a slow process, my right ankle rebounded and the muscle tone eventually returned to my calf. By the beginning of my senior season, about nine months after my initial injury had occurred, I felt stronger physically from head to toe than I ever had in my seventeen years of life. Yet, mentally, I still wasn't sure whether I could come back and pitch with the same domination that I'd demonstrated during my first three years at Monte Vista High. I felt so much pressure on me. There were so many unanswered questions and doubts that still filled my brain, like weeds in a garden. I knew that if I wanted to be successful I had to cleanse these negative thoughts completely.

Victoria had just the right solution. Since I only had five periods of school during my senior year, I would go down on the field all by myself during sixth period. Before every home game I would repaint the bases, the pitcher's mound and home plate with bright white paint. Moving the brush back and forth was like therapy as I prepared my mental game plan for each opponent. I know it sounds silly, but the ritual actually worked. For a few minutes, my mind was focused on the strokes of my brush rather than the pressures of success or failure. Painting was simple and relaxing. In fact, it worked so well to calm my nerves that a couple of games into the season I put a paintbrush in my duffel bag for road games.

Everyone thought I was crazy as I swished it back and forth through the air for close to an hour on some bus rides.

Any skepticism that haunted me about my ability vanished when we opened our season 6-0. I was the winning pitcher in four of those six games, and twice I shut our opponents out completely. My pitching arm was stronger than ever due to the weightlifting I had done during my rehab. Plus, after spending such a long time in a cast, I had become very aware of the use of my legs as they related to pitching. Victoria had been preaching this to me since our first lesson, but it never sunk in until I was forced to practice pitching without them. During my first pitching appearance after my rehab I began to use my legs much more efficiently. Strangely, I was throwing the ball much harder than I had in the past. This was a very unexpected benefit of my injury. Suddenly, I was a true power pitcher, throwing the ball faster than any other pitcher in our section.

Our team finally lost a game after winning our first six, but then we blazed right into another streak, finishing victorious in nine of the next eleven games for an amazing 15-3 record. We were first in our league and a sure bet to make the playoffs with just three games left.

In those final games we hit some bumps as injuries mounted. Our first baseman Roselee Rivera broke her pinky finger diving back to the bag to make a barehanded tag. We also lost our starting right fielder, Marcia Dunson, after she contracted mono halfway through the year. And in our season finale, which we lost, I twisted my right ankle when I tangled feet with the first baseman on a close play. I left the game, iced my ankle for several hours, and barely slept that night as I imagined the worst case scenario: another injury and an end to my senior season.

Thankfully, my ankle bounced back quickly from the sprain. Even though our team finished 15-6 and lost our chance at a regular season title, our phenomenal start allowed us to earn a spot in the county playoffs. Despite our team's great success, college coaches rarely frequented our games. My injury, coupled with the small town I lived in, were both reasons why they stayed away. It really made me sad at times. I knew I was good enough to pitch in college and I knew that if I got the chance, I could really help a college team. I also knew that paying tuition was going to be hard on Dad. He had promised me he would find a way to send me—and I believed him—but I wanted so badly to get that scholarship. I desperately wanted to give him that gift.

With Victoria's constant encouragement, I remained upbeat about the empty seats in the stands, heeding her advice to seize the moment and maximize the enjoyment of my final season. Sometimes, after a game, the situation weighed heavily on me. I wished a thousand times that I had never run that race against LuAnn. I knew that if I hadn't my life would be different right now. That thought was very frustrating. Once in awhile, I'd stay in the lockerroom by myself for a half hour or so, pondering why I was still being overlooked and wondering what I needed to do to catch somebody's attention. I nearly drove myself mad.

Once the playoffs began, I put all those negative thoughts out of my mind. This was my last chance to show anybody who was watching what kind of player I was. We got off to a great start as our bats and gloves shined in a first-round 10-2 win. In the quarterfinals, with a rested ankle, I took care of business on the mound, hurling a four-hitter in a 6-1 victory. We faced our toughest test in the semis, but prevailed 3-2 over our rivals, the Del Ray Cougars. That set up a showdown against Ponderosa High, with the winner taking home the prestigious County Championship Cup—a trophy Monte Vista High had never won.

When the last game of my high school career finally arrived on a sweltering hot day at the beginning of June, I had given up worrying. All that was left to do was go out a winner and let the chips fall where they may.

Victoria asked the maintenance crew at the Dawn Community College field if I could arrive a couple of hours before the game and maintain my pregame ritual of painting the bases. They obliged, welcoming the lessening of their workload. I'd gotten my driver's license a year earlier and Victoria allowed me to take her car to the field three hours before the game. As I lifted the bucket of paint out of her trunk and made my way onto the field, I immediately recognized the weight dangling from my right arm. No, the paint can wasn't any heavier that day than on other game days, but the do-or-die nature of the championship game got me thinking about the burden my right arm carried. The intense pressure and responsibility placed on my pitching arm for this title game could only be put into words one way—this game and this performance meant everything to us.

When I reached the field I started painting first base—then second and third base in sequence. With each stroke of the brush I visualized myself connecting for a single, a double, a triple—rounding each of the bases, pumping my arms, sliding, diving, jumping and winning. Then I took the paint can and brush to the mound. As I glossed over the worn rubber, I pictured myself dragging my right foot and exploding off the mound with my left. I imagined each of my pitches, hot fastballs, sick curves, dramatic drops, quick rises and confusing changeups, all coming off my hand smoothly as I finished with an uplifting follow through.

My last project was to polish up home plate. There, I visualized batters frozen in their stance as fastballs whizzed by them. I pictured hitters swinging helplessly through a deadly drop, and sluggers flailing ahead of deceiving changeups.

Minutes before the game started, I relieved my nerves by swishing my cleats across the many drops of paint I'd spilled in the dirt earlier. Then, I shocked all of my teammates, and even myself, when I dug inside my bag and pulled out some gold and maroon hair ribbons. Ribbons and bows were a part of my history—a history that ended when Mom passed away. I stared at the ribbons for a few seconds, taking a moment to breathe.

I hollered down the bench to my fashion-friendly teammate, Liz Williams, who always wore lots of makeup and looked pretty on game days. "Hey Lizzy, can you give me one of your high-style braid jobs?"

Every one of my teammates froze in their tracks and stared at me. They knew the reason for my free-flowing hair. Ever since Mom died, I refused to wear bows, ribbons or even ponytails. Even though my hair got in the way and blew out of control at times, my teammates understood my reluctance to revisit the deep memory tied to my mom and my long locks.

"I want the works, Lizzy." I spoke clearly, and Lizzy walked toward me.

As Lizzy braided my hair, Victoria came by. "I guess Superestrella Cinderella is in order today, huh?" Victoria had learned of my Bobby Sox nickname at my quinceañera. Until today, she had no reason to use the nickname.

After Liz had tied the final knot, I huddled all the players around me in front of the dugout and provided one inspiring remark: "We own this field, guys. Let's play like it."

I ran out to the mound with a spring in my step, feeling lighter and freer and much less scratchy on my neck. I hadn't worn my hair like this since the first time I ever pitched. That was nearly seven years ago now. When I reached the rubber, I heard a familiar clanking sound amidst the cheers and whistles. My heart raced and I glanced toward the stands as if Mom were sitting in the front row shaking her soda can. Instead, I noticed my dad, sitting with my brothers, and *he* was shaking Mom's rock-filled soda can and screaming, "Go Selena, go! Go Selena, go!"

Slightly embarrassed, I bowed my head in appreciation of my family. I glanced over to the crowd one last time and spotted Jason Lebot, the coach from the College of the Pines. I didn't recognize any other college coaches in the stands. Seeing him there made my heart jump for a moment, but then I calmed down. I was determined to let nothing—not even the question of college—interfere with this special moment in my life. My final high school softball game would deplete all of my strength, consume all of my positive energy, and employ all of my skill and determination. I'd leave everything out on the field.

Ready, locked and loaded, I zeroed in on LuAnn's large catcher's glove as the first Ponderosa batter stepped to the plate. I tucked my right elbow in, pulled my shoulders back, made a deep bend at the knees and, with all my might, windmilled the game's first pitch. The fastest ball I'd ever thrown buzzed right down the middle of the strike zone, leaving the hitter looking like a statue. I followed with a sharp rise and then a baffling changeup, needing just three pitches to record my first strikeout.

I fanned eight more batters in the next five innings, finding an unbelievable groove. Almost every time my hand released the ball, it snapped LuAnn's glove without her needing to flinch an inch. I felt like a fighter pilot using radar to land pinpoint placement missiles.

Unfortunately, like Ponderosa, our bats were silent. Heading into the top of the seventh inning, we faced a scoreless tie. Ponderosa brought up the top of its order, and for the first time in the championship game, I walked the leadoff batter. I'd allowed just two hits in the entire game so far. Fortunately, the next two batters in the inning grounded out, leaving a runner on first base with two outs.

Ponderosa depended on its cleanup hitter to come through for them. She'd collected both of their hits—each on outside drop pitches. So when LuAnn signaled for an inside fastball, I nodded my head in agreement. The Ponderosa slugger grunted as she swung at the first offering, ripping a sharp grounder to our star shortstop, Jenni DelCruz, who was positioned perfectly in the hole. Unfortunately, the hard shot went through Jenni's legs and rolled into the left centerfield gap.

The runner at first base had left the bag before I tossed the pitch to the plate, so by the time the ball skirted through Jenni's legs, she was already rounding second. Amazingly, as the ball reached our center fielder, Suzie Dime, the runner was on her way home. Lynda scooped up the ball and threw a laser beam home, beating the runner by ten feet. LuAnn applied the tag, and with a sigh of relief our Monarch team sprinted off the field, hoping to win the title trophy in our last at bat. But to our surprise, the umpires all conferred around second base and within minutes called our team back on the field. They ruled that our shortstop had interfered with the Ponderosa runner as she ran from second base to third base. We were all stunned as we made our way back onto the field.

Staring up at the scoreboard from the pitcher's mound, I saw that Ponderosa had been awarded a run due to the interference. They took a 1-0 lead.

Victoria sprinted out onto the field and displayed an anger I've never seen from her before. I couldn't hear what she was saying from the pitcher's mound, but her index finger pointing everywhere and her bright red face indicated the heated nature of her words. Victoria left the field shaking her head in disagreement as she gathered us together along the first-base line. "Don't let the umpires take this game from you! Let's get one more out and finish this thing off with our bats."

Furious with the umpires, I took a minute to cool down behind the mound, fixing my visor back on my head. A moment earlier, I had replaced my visor with a batting helmet in the dugout, thinking the inning was over. So after tightening my fancy ribbons, I looked into LuAnn's glove and refocused again.

First pitch, fastball, strike one.

Second pitch, curveball, strike two.

Third pitch, drop ball outside, strike three, side retired—again.

Our dugout bellowed with chatter as the top of the order faced our final chance at a championship. Now it was payback time! Our leadoff batter, Marla Montez, approached the plate. Just three pitches later, Marla slap-bunted a single in between short and third. This sent our crowd into a frenzy as the throw to first base wasn't even close.

Our number two hitter popped out before I stepped to the plate for an opportunity to get revenge. Prior to digging my cleats into the batter's box, I knelt down to tighten my shoelaces. I - adjusted my Jose Valentine batting gloves and my black-and-white striped wristbands—the same wristbands I'd worn since Bobby Sox.

I went 1-for-3 in earlier at-bats, pulling a changeup down the third baseline for my only hit. Using a pitcher's mentality, I expected an outside fastball on the first pitch of this at-bat, figuring the Ponderosa pitcher believed I couldn't catch up to it. Prepared, I choked up a bit and decided to go with the pitch. Sure enough, the heater headed for the outside half of the plate. Utilizing a compact swing, I lined a shot the opposite way into the right-center gap. Our leadoff hitter, Marla Montez, raced all the way home from first as I sailed into second base, jubilantly clapping my hands in celebration of the 1-1 tie.

With one out, our cleanup hitter, Jill Hart, stepped up to the plate, hoping to deliver the knockout blow. At 6-feet, 160-pounds, her frame alone intimidated opponents. Jill had a reputation for her power, but in this at-bat, she suffered a power outage, striking out on three straight pitches.

So with one chance left, our championship destiny fell on the shoulders of LuAnn Gores, the girl I had raced against and lost, in a big way. LuAnn and I had become even closer friends since my accident and I felt excited that she was at the plate. I believed in her, not only because she was such a gifted athlete, but because she carried herself with such confidence. In a high-pressure situation like this one, she was the perfect person to have up there.

Before the first pitch, I surveyed the outfield, noticing the center fielder shading over into the left-centerfield gap. With two outs, I knew I could get a good jump off second base because I would be running on contact. I also figured Victoria, being the gambler she was, would wave me home if there was any chance I could score. Not that I was planning on acting on my assumptions. I would wait and follow Victoria's instructions.

LuAnn's keen eye, which is very typical for a catcher who sits behind the plate on defense all game, helped her march ahead in the count 2-0. The next pitch was pivotal. The Ponderosa pitcher delivered a fastball right down the middle of the plate. LuAnn teed off on this pitch as if she knew what was coming, lining the heater back up the middle just out of the reach of Ponderosa's second baseman.

Breaking on the ping of the bat, I headed for third base. My eyes focused on Victoria, who stood a fourth of the way down the line. Just before I stepped on the third-base bag, she ferociously waved me home. "Go! Go! Go!" She shouted.

As I sprinted toward the plate I noticed Ponderosa's catcher attempting to block my path. For an instant, I imagined sliding right foot first into the fully geared catcher and the collision causing the agony of a re-injured ankle. Within a blink of an eye, that fear disappeared and I descended naturally into an aggressive slide, leading with my right leg and following with my bent left knee.

I reached the plate just as the catcher pulled down the throw, attempting to tag my chest. The force of my momentum jolted the catcher backwards. She sprawled to the ground, along with her mask and my helmet. The throw had beaten me home, but the collision caused the ball to drop out of her glove and land loosely on the ground.

"Safe! Safe! Safe!" yelled the umpire as he frantically waved his arms across his body.

Before I could ascend from the dust, my teammates jumped on top of me. We formed a huge heap of hysterical teenage girls right there on home plate. Although the weight pressing on my sprawled-out body felt heavy, my excitement numbed me to any pain. I was safe at home, and we were number one!

CHAPTER TEN

SAFE AT HOME

As LuAnn and I walked to the locker-room, ten minutes after our dog pile at the plate, we laughed about how nervous we both were in our final at-bats. We also talked about the excitement of having just one more day of high school remaining. LuAnn was going to attend Mammoth College in Tucson, just a two-hour drive from our hometown. Although she had not gotten a scholarship, the coach of the basketball team had all but guaranteed her a spot on the squad. Silently I sulked, knowing that I had just twenty-four hours to sign a college scholarship, which was about as likely as getting struck by lightning at this point.

When LuAnn and I passed by Victoria's office window, I could see her sitting at her desk across from a man wearing a forest green baseball cap. Just as LuAnn and I pushed open the locker-room door, Victoria hollered at me from her office. "Selena, I need to see you for a minute."

I patted LuAnn on the back and walked over to Victoria. When I reached her office, she put her hand on my shoulder and guided me through the door. "Someone's here to see you." Victoria spoke excitedly and right away I felt that something was up—*but what?*

Just as I walked into her small office the man stood up and turned around to face me. To my delight, it was Coach Jason Lebot from the College of the Pines. He was the only Coach who'd expressed any interest in me. Coach Jason greeted me with a hearty handshake. Having already met, there wasn't any need for introductions. Coach Jason's warm smile was infectious, forcing me to grin, too.

"You played a great game out there, Selena!" He said.

I responded to his compliment, shaking my head humbly. "Thank you very much." Although my mouth spoke these words, my brain was temporarily out of order. I simply could not focus on this conversation—not until I knew what he was doing in Victoria's office. This thought, and this thought alone, buzzed through me like an electric shock. Before I could glance over at Victoria's desk to look for any sign of scholarship papers, Coach Jason interjected, "So what are your plans for celebrating the big win?"

Celebrating the big win? I thought. *What does that matter? Does he mean celebrate because it is my last win?* My heart continued racing, wondering what was happening. *Why was he in Victoria's office? Why had she called me in here?* "I'm not sure." I answered, "My dad's supposed to meet me up here in a few minutes, so maybe he'll have something planned." I was barely paying attention to the words that flowed from my mouth.

Coach Jason took a step closer to me. "Well, that's great. Maybe he'd like to be here when I ask you to sign a full-ride softball scholarship to the College of the Pines."

"Yeah maybe." I stopped myself, unsure of what I had just heard. "Wait, what did you just say?" I smiled from ear to ear, realizing exactly what he had said.

Coach Lebot repeated himself anyway, "I said, maybe he'd like to be here when I ask you to sign a full-ride softball scholarship to the College of the Pines." He spoke those words again and I half-screamed, half-laughed and half-cried at the top of my lungs in excitement.

Dad arrived right on cue at Victoria's door. He took his hat off as he entered, shaking hands with Coach Lebot. "What's all the yelping about?" Dad asked with a look of confused excitement on his face.

Victoria addressed him with a handshake-turned-hug. "Hi Mr. Garcia." She then pointed in my direction. "Selena has something to tell you."

I turned and looked Dad in the eyes, as mine welled up with tears. "Dad, I'm going to college. I'm going to play softball on a scholarship. It's all free!"

Dad was silent at first. Then he grabbed a chair and sat down. I had never seen him look so happy or so proud. "You did it," he whispered. "I can't believe what you did." He stared directly into my eyes when he said, "You don't quit, Selena. You're just like your mother." He kissed me on the forehead and sat back down, laughing.

I would cherish those words and that moment forever.

The car ride home that afternoon was so much fun. Dad was driving and Joe was sitting in the front seat with Carlos and I in the back. We left the parking lot and Dad kept shouting out the window, "My baby's going to college!" As usual, I was embarrassed. Joe and Carlos were shaking Mom's rock-filled soda can and the music was blasting. We must have looked like a bunch of crazy people as we exited the parking lot. I don't think I'd ever smiled so big.

When we got back to our apartment Joe and Carlos were still full of energy and asked me if I wanted to head down to the Field for a catch. Needless to say, I was surprised by the offer, especially because it came from Joe. We hadn't all played catch together in a long time and I probably hadn't been on the Field in close to three years. Playing softball all the time, and training at school hadn't left much time for backyard games.

We grabbed our mitts and a baseball that had been chewed up by Campeona, and left the house just before the sun began to set. When we got down to the Field I had to laugh. Joe was bossing Carlos and me around the same way he did when were eight and nine years old. "Carlos, you stand by first base. Selena, you line up by home plate." He looked up at the sun, which was beginning to set. "Hurry up." Some things never changed.

We played catch together for about thirty minutes as the sun faded in the background. It was the perfect end to the perfect day: I was going to college, Dad wasn't going to be burdened with a giant tuition bill, we had won the championship game, and I was back on the Field, revisiting all the amazing memories of my childhood and playing catch with my brothers. As usual, the only thing that was missing was Mom.

Carlos threw a laser at me, and the pop of my mitt echoed across the diamond. The echo was familiar, but it was a noise I hadn't heard in a long time—I couldn't remember the last time I had thrown a *baseball*.

You see, the popping sound of a softball hitting the center of a mitt is totally different. When a softball lands in your glove, the pop is more hollow and seems to last longer than the quick pop of a baseball. Plus, it's preceded by a low *whoosh,* as the larger ball makes more contact with the leather glove before settling deep in its pocket. These two different sounds represented two distinct stages in my life and, for the first time, each sound was completely distinguishable from the other. I tossed the baseball over to Joe as hard as I could.

He laughed, "Jeez, Selena, you've got one heck of an arm."

It was at that moment, listening to Joe compliment me, that I truly began to appreciate how much my life had changed over the years. And it was at that moment when I realized how strange a baseball felt in my hand. It was tiny and hard and heavy. When I threw it, the feeling was foreign to me. I remembered the first time I'd ever thrown a softball at Bobby Sox practice. I hated it. The ball felt big and soft and light. I had wondered how I would ever be able to throw it with the accuracy I could throw a baseball. I never imagined myself getting accustomed to that giant ball. Here I was, years later, holding a tiny and strange ball in my hands, realizing that my transformation into a softball player was complete.

My eyes glanced all over the Field as we continued to toss the baseball back and forth around the diamond. The dimensions of the Field were exactly the same as when I was a kid, only everything looked smaller. I laughed when I looked at the parked cars a few feet from right field, the splintery wood fence, and the giant holes dotting the outfield. "How did we ever play on this field?" I asked my brothers.

Carlos had the perfect answer, "Why did we ever stop?"

That final summer at home passed by quicker than any summer before it. Three and a half months after that final game, with Dad's old pickup stuffed with bags, bats and boxes, we began the long trip to Utah, the site of my home for the next four years. Dad had volunteered to drive me. Although Joe and Carlos offered to come along, there was no room for them in the packed truck.

Instead, we said goodbye in the family room. Joe and Carlos, who were both attending community college nearby, offered me hugs and brotherly advice ranging from, "Stay away from the boys" to "Keep your eye on the ball."

I pulled Joe off the old, tan corduroy couch first. He got serious for a second, which had hardly ever happened: "If you have any problems with any of the guys over there, you just let me know." Joe was covering up any signs of sadness with his typical macho attitude. "I'll be up there that day if you need me." He smiled, "I'll miss you, girl," then he gave me a kiss on the cheek, lifting me off the ground in his arms.

Carlos got up from the couch next and offered a hearty embrace, too. In his sensitive manner, he whispered softly in my ear, "I'm gonna miss you, too. Who's gonna sit between me and Jose at the dinner table now?" I tried not to cry when Carlos made this comment. "Don't forget to call us." He kissed my cheek too, and Dad and I left the house.

With tears in my eyes, I left my home for the greatest adventure of my life.

Dad and I drove to the gas station to fill up before dropping by Victoria's house. Although I felt overjoyed at my upcoming journey, I couldn't hide the deep sadness I was experiencing by leaving her behind. With little time to spare, I sat next to Victoria on her couch and thanked her over and over again for her guidance, her advice, her encouragement and her friendship.

Victoria held me tight and whispered in my ear, "Selena, you've shown more courage than anyone else I've met in my life. I love you, sister."

I reached in my pocket and pulled out an envelope. "You can open it, but read my letter later, after I leave."

Victoria ripped the envelope and pulled out a prepaid, twenty-dollar gas card, which was all I could afford. I smiled. "Now you have no excuse not to come visit me for our first game."

Victoria walked to her kitchen table and grabbed the handles of a brown paper grocery bag, setting the heavy item on my lap. I looked inside and lugged out a giant box of laundry detergent. Also inside was a brand-new box of stationary. Smiling, she said: "I figured you'd need both those things."

She handed me a letter too, tucked inside an envelope. Taped to the front was a prepaid phone card. She shook her finger at me. "Now you have no excuse not to call me!" I laughed, thinking about how odd—and yet how similar—our gifts to one another were. We truly were sisters.

We hugged again and I cried as we said goodbye. Victoria tried to soften the separation. "I'll be at your first weekend fall tournament, I promise."

Victoria waved at us as we pulled out of her driveway and made our way toward the final stop on my goodbye tour, the top of Eternal Mountain, the burial site of my mother. As we walked in between the tombstones, I started to get emotional right away. When we reached Mom's plot, I knelt down and lost it, crying hard for a moment before regaining my composure. With Dad standing a few feet behind me, I rubbed my hand across her name—Maria Nora Garcia. I put a flower on the top of her stone and sat on the soft grass. Dad sat next to me.

"I know you're with me, Mom." I reached inside my backpack and pulled out a couple of items: the hair ribbon I wore in the County Championship game, a copy of the newspaper article from that game, and the large ball point pen I used to sign on the dotted line for my scholarship. I laid the mementos beside her stone. "I know you're proud of me, too." I wiped away a tear. "I can't wait to see what happens next. I know it's going to be a lot different, but I'm ready." I kissed my palm as tears ran down my face and gently laid the wet hand on her tombstone. "I still love you." I spoke the truth. I did still love her. You see, that's the thing about death—it can't take away your memories and it can't take away your love. It took me a long time to realize that.

After Dad said a few words to Mom we made our way back toward the car. The first hour or so of that trip was totally silent. I think we were both deeply affected by visiting Mom's grave. Eventually though, we loosened up and had some great talks.

The journey to Rising Road, Utah, was long but it went by quickly. Hours and hours of Dad going over my schedule, giving me advice, and talking about my new life made the trip go very fast. I'd never heard him talk so much! It was like *he* was going to college! Before I knew it, we were only fifteen minutes away, rolling through the northern part of Arizona and into Utah.

Before we arrived at the school, Dad had one more thing to say. "Selena, you're the first person in our family to go to a four-year college—and on a scholarship!" Dad slapped my leg in excitement, then paused. "I know I haven't been able to buy you a lot of things or take you a lot of places, Selena. I wish I could have done more for you guys." He paused, "Your mother, if she were here—"

I cut Dad off, "If she were here she would be so proud of you, Dad. You kept our family together." There was more I wanted to say to Dad, but as the car continued to make its way toward Pines Road, there was nothing to say but, "Wow, there it is!"

We both stared in awe at the beautiful buildings that stood before us. The college was even more impressive than I had imagined. I pointed out my window at the signature clock tower emerging from the center of campus. I'd never seen the school in person, I'd only flipped through pictures in the brochure Coach had sent me.

We pulled up to the security gate and asked for directions to the athletics department. After weaving though brick buildings and fraternity houses, we found the facility and located Coach Lebot's office. Excited, I knocked on his door to say hello.

"Hi, Selena!" Coach Lebot emerged from the doorway and extended his hand. "Glad you made it here safely."

Coach took us on a tour of the facility. Although it was not a top twenty program, College of the Pines did compete at the Division 1 level—the highest level college sports had to offer. We passed by the campus trophy case, loaded with conference title plaques. We then entered the state-of-the-art weight room. I figured I'd be frequenting this space often, especially since I'd learned about the value of exercise during my ankle injury rehab.

Next, Coach used his keys to open the softball locker-room.

The beautiful carpeted area was bordered by lockers, each painted in a bright forest green. Hanging in each locker was a vibrant white jersey. I walked to the nearest stall and turned the uniform to the backside. "GARCIA 31" was stitched on it. Of course, I started crying again. I couldn't contain my excitement. I was living in a dream, but it was real. "This is so cool!" I said.

I remembered the day I walked through the Arizona Scorpions locker-room and was in awe at the professional players' gear. That day I had dreamed of finding my name glistening across a locker stall—that dream had become a reality.

We exited the building and headed outside for our final destination, Forest Field. The frigid night weather of the fall season immediately sent goose bumps down my body. I had become accustomed to the sweltering heat of Arizona. Anytime the weather dropped below sixty-five degrees, I got the chills. I quickly concluded that with my move to Utah I'd be experiencing entirely different weather, and would actually get the chance to see snow! I was just beginning to grasp how different my life was about to become.

I slipped my hands into the side pockets of my jacket, wondering how far we'd walk before spotting the diamond. Two minutes later Coach Jason stopped us. "Go ahead and walk right up that little bank of stairs. The field is at the top. I'm gonna go right over here and turn on the lights."

My heart was racing as we reached the top step. Then— like a bolt of lightning—the bright lights flashed on all around me. I blinked my eyes a few times, adjusting to the brilliance. *Whoa*, I thought. When I finally regained focus, I dropped my jaw in wonder. Lush green grass in the outfield *and* the infield! A padded wall!

Real red brick clay! Cement dugouts with heated seats! A true bullpen covered for shade! *Two* batting cages with lights! A press box and an electronic scoreboard with video replay! "Whoa," I said aloud as I looked over at Dad.

I started to think about the Field in Tierra de Sueño, and sitting on top of the big rock, desperately attempting to get myself into a game. Now look at me—this was *really* the big time.

"So what do you think, Selena?" Coach Jason smiled.

"It's amazing. I've never seen anything like it." I spoke without looking away from the field.

Dad laughed and shook Coach Jason's hand again, thanking him for this opportunity for his only daughter.

Coach continued, "You guys are welcome to stay down here for as long as you'd like. I've got to finish up some paperwork in the office, but I'll see you back here tomorrow for the first team meeting."

"You got it Coach." I nodded my head and grinned. "Thanks for showing us around."

Dad was hungry from the long ride and left at the same time as Coach to pick up some takeout for the two of us. I wanted to stay at the field awhile longer, so Dad agreed to come back and get me in an hour. As I sat in the dugout, I noticed a softball tucked in the corner under the bench. I strolled over and picked it up, reading the words C.O.P., for College of the Pines, faintly written across it. As I rubbed it in my hands, I noticed the pristinely groomed mound area in the middle of the diamond and decided to walk out there.

Before reaching the rubber I removed my red jacket and tied it to the backstop fence behind home plate. It hung in what would be the heart of the strike zone. Arriving at the mound, I pulled off my mom's ring from my right ring finger and put it in my jeans pocket. I placed my feet across the strip and set the ball in my right hand. As I eyed my red jacket, I paused, taking in the silence surrounding me.

This rare quiet moment led me to ponder the past eighteen years of my life and the loss I had experienced. Mom's death had left a huge void in me, a hole that would never be filled. Then my ankle injury cost me all but one of my scholarship opportunities. Through it all, I gained so much. The people I met and everything I went through gave me a much better appreciation for life.

I reached my hand into the back pocket of my pants and pulled out Mom's picture. I kissed it softly, knowing that Mom was with me at that very moment. Peering in toward home plate, I crouched down and pretended to see the catcher's sign. Like I'd done a thousand times before, I began to rock backwards slightly. My eyes narrowed and my arm windmilled around. Then I pushed forward with my legs, using all my might. With an upward follow-through, I flung the worn ball to the backstop. The rapidly spinning sphere smacked the heart of the jacket.

Instantly, I felt right at home.

TEST YOURSELF...ARE YOU A PROFESSIONAL READER?

Chapter 1: The Field

Describe The Field.

Why weren't errors tolerated in right field at The Field?

Besides an automatic invitation to The Field, what was the greatest reward Selena earned when she defeated Joe in the home run derby?

ESSAY

Until Selena thought up a plan, she wasn't even allowed to compete in the home run derby. How did this make her feel? Write about a time in your life when you were excluded. How did you feel?

Chapter 2: A Hard Call

Why didn't Selena want to play softball with the girls?

Name one aspect of playing baseball with the boys that Selena didn't enjoy.

What was the team's reaction to Selena's amazing double play? How did this reaction make her feel?

ESSAY

In this chapter, it becomes obvious that Selena is underappreciated by her teammates. Describe a situation in your life when you felt you didn't receive the recognition you deserved.

Chapter 3: A Changeup

What are a few reasons Selena enjoyed the switch from baseball to softball?

Why was Selena's mom so thrilled that Selena was enjoying her time on the softball team?

What was Selena's nickname? How did she acquire such a nickname?

ESSAY

In Chapter 3, Selena shows that your attitude can affect your performance. Describe a situation in your life when you mentally convinced yourself you could do something, and then did it. Why are positive thoughts so important?

Chapter 4: A Goodnight Kiss

What did Selena's mother mean by the expression "when you get lemons, you make lemonade"?

Why did Selena sometimes feel unlucky that she was a girl?

What seemed important to Selena after her mother passed away?

ESSAY

What do you think Selena's mother means by saying "that things never work out the way you plan them"? Give an example from your life of something not working out the way that you planned, yet eventually working out anyhow.

Chapter 5: A Challenge

During this chapter, Selena reads thirty-four books in four weeks. Why?

What was the "coolest" room that Selena has ever seen? Describe this room.

Why did Carla select number thirty-one when Joe Valentine asked all the kids to pick a number between one and 100?

ESSAY

Joe Valentine is shown as a role model to Selena in Chapter 5. What is a role model? Name someone in your life who has motivated you to achieve great things. Describe how this person helped you.

Chapter 6: Nobody's Perfect

When Selena returned to softball, what newly developed skill of hers shocked her teammates?

Why did Selena keep a picture of her mom in her back pocket when she took the mound?

Who was Victoria Joyce? What achievement of Selena's grabbed Victoria's attention?

ESSAY

Selena accomplishes a tremendous feat in this chapter by tossing a no-hitter. Detail a personal award, accomplishment, or honor in your life that makes you the most proud. Why are you so proud of this achievement?

Chapter 7: A Bumpy Ride

What life experiences did Selena and Victoria share that further strengthened their bond?

Give an example of how Coach Moody managed "by the book."

How did the softball team do under Coach Moody's direction?

ESSAY

In Chapter 7, Selena doesn't listen to Coach Moody and disrespects her in the process. Eventually, she learns to treat Coach Moody with respect, even though she doesn't always agree with her. Detail an example in your life when you disrespected someone. What lesson did you learn from it? Why is it important to respect people?

Chapter 8: Two Surprises

What is a quinceañera?

Why was Selena so excited about the news of the replacement softball coach?

What "tool" helped Selena the most in dealing with the pressures of playing softball?

ESSAY

Selena exhibits her resolve by not quitting the softball team in this chapter. Have you ever quit something in your life? Explain what happened. Why is finishing something you have started so important?

Chapter 9: Cinderella Superestrella

How did Selena hurt her ankle?

What lesson about pitching did Selena learn during her ankle rehabilitation?

Why did Selena refuse to wear her hair in bows, ribbons, or in a ponytail after her mother died?

ESSAY

In Chapter 9, when Selena injures her ankle, she manages to turn a bad situation into something positive. In fact, she becomes a more complete softball player after her injury. Detail a time in your life when you turned a negative situation into a positive one. What did you learn about yourself?

Chapter 10: Safe at Home

What news did Coach Lebot deliver to Selena in Victoria's office?

When was Selena's transformation to the sport of softball officially complete?

What did Selena leave beside her mother's tombstone when she visited the burial site?

ESSAY

Congratulations! You have completed another Scobre Press book! After joining Selena on her journey, detail what you learned from her life and experiences. How are you going to use Selena's story to help you achieve your dreams? What character traits does Selena have that could help you to overcome obstacles in your life?